wedlock cake murder

A Maple Hills Cozy Mystery - 12

wendy meadows

Majestic Owl Publishing LLC
P.O. Box 997
Newport, NH 03773

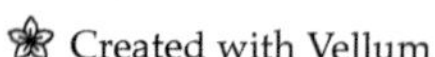 Created with Vellum

chapter one

The cool air blew through the trees and sent the colorful leaves spinning toward the ground. One leaf blew around and landed on a shop window. Inside the shop, Nikki and her friends were busy planning her wedding. Nikki's wedding was only a week away, and she was tying up loose ends and designing her cake.

"Are you sure you want to design your own cake?" Lidia asked. One of Nikki's best friends, Lidia was older than Nikki and worked at the chocolate shop.

Nikki smiled. "Absolutely," she replied. Nikki owned the chocolate shop. She had moved to Maple Hills with her son, Seth, after her husband walked out on her. Her husband had reappeared but was now in custody in another town. Nikki was excited to be marrying her beau, Hawk. Hawk was a local detective whom Nikki helped occasionally. They had solved a few mysteries together and had grown closer and eventually fell in love. Hawk asked Nikki to marry him a few months ago. Nikki gave him an enthusiastic yes, and they agreed that they did not need a long engagement. Nikki also did not want a big wedding. Lidia would be her maid of honor, and Seth was the best man. A handful of guests were invited to the wedding, but Seth had convinced Nikki to have a larger reception afterward. Seth and his girlfriend, Tori, offered to help with the catering and music.

"All you have to do is show up," Seth told Nikki. Nikki agreed to the reception but had insisted on designing and baking the cake.

"I am an award-winning chocolatier, after all." Nikki smiled at Lidia, Seth, and Tori, and they laughed. Nikki had won an exclusive chocolate-making contest the year before, and people in the town would not let her live it down. Nikki had wanted to put the trophy in her attic, but Seth insisted she display it in the store. They compromised, and the award was now behind the counter. Nikki looked at her drawing. It would be a difficult cake to pull off, but Nikki knew she could do it.

"Your drawings look amazing," Tori exclaimed. She also worked at the chocolate shop with Nikki. Seth had also once worked there, but he was now on the police force. Hawk's father, Chief Daily, hired him.

"Thank you, Tori," Nikki replied. She drew a semicircle on the page and was about to show them another idea when the front door of the store opened.

"Hey, Hawk," Seth said and stepped between Hawk and the table. Nikki quickly put away her designs and got up. She walked around the table and gave Hawk a hug and kiss. Hawk was tall and handsome, his rugged looks and great personality had easily won Nikki over. He hugged Nikki and said hello to the gang.

"What are you hiding from me?" Hawk asked.

"Nothing, why?" Nikki replied, trying to hide a smile.

"You know you can't keep things from me," Hawk said. "I am a detective, after all."

Nikki laughed. "It's a surprise for the wedding, silly," she said, squeezing Hawk's arm. "Don't try to figure it out."

"Okay," Hawk agreed. They sat down at a small table and Lidia brought them some hot chocolate.

"So, what kind of new creations are you making?" Hawk asked Nikki. Nikki enjoyed making seasonal candies along with her regular offerings.

"I am making maple walnut leaves in different colors for the fall," Nikki said. "Would you like to try one?"

"Sure," Hawk replied. Nikki got up and went to the kitchen in the back of the store. She took out a tray of candies from the refrigerator and pulled a couple off the tray. She put them on a plate and carried them back to Hawk. She sat down as Hawk tried the maple leaf candies.

"Wow, these are delicious," Hawk said.

"Thank you," Nikki replied. The door opened again, and a customer walked in. Lidia took care of him while Nikki and Hawk talked.

"Are you ready for the big day?" Nikki asked Hawk.

"Yep," Hawk said. "Are you?"

"Nope," Nikki teased. Hawk laughed. They had agreed on a simple wedding in the park. The mayor would marry them, and Captain Daily would walk Nikki down the aisle. Nikki would carry a simple bouquet that the florist was creating for her, and Hawk would have a boutonniere for his lapel. Those were the only flowers for the wedding. There would be no candles, just minimal decorations. Nikki was glad she and Hawk had agreed on the wedding plans. Nikki smiled as Hawk sipped his hot chocolate. She was happy and excited about the wedding. Because the plans were minimal, it was a more relaxing preparation. Nikki had helped plan a few weddings while she lived in Maple Hills, and she knew what she wanted and did not want. Some weddings had been elaborate, and some were simple. The brides in the simple weddings seemed more relaxed to Nikki, so she went that route.

"What are you thinking about?" Hawk asked Nikki.

"I was remembering some weddings I helped plan and

provided chocolates for," Nikki replied. "Remember the mayor's daughter's wedding?"

"How can I forget?" Hawk replied. "Aside from the dead body at the reception, it was lovely." Nikki scowled at Hawk and then laughed. She had helped Hawk solve that mystery, and it had turned her off of elaborate weddings. The mayor had insisted on marrying Hawk and Nikki when he found out they were engaged. He appreciated all of their help with the investigation. He had also offered his mansion as a stage for the wedding or the reception. Nikki thanked him and took him up on his offer for the reception. The mayor was happy, and that meant the chief and Hawk would be happy, which meant Nikki was happy.

"Have Seth and Tori got the catering figured out?" Hawk asked. "If not, I can probably help them."

"Did I hear my name?" Seth asked. He had been behind the counter helping Tori. It was his day off and he enjoyed spending time at the chocolate shop, especially when Tori was there. Seth walked over to the table and joined Hawk and Nikki. A couple more customers walked in, and Lidia took care of them.

"Hawk wants to know if you need help with the catering," Nikki told Seth.

"We have it covered, but thank you," Seth replied.

"Okay. Just let me know if you need anything," Hawk said. Seth thanked him and then got up and went back to the counter to assist Tori.

"Would you like to take a walk in the park?" Hawk asked Nikki. Nikki looked around. The customers were taken care of, and she wanted to stretch her legs. Besides, she always enjoyed spending time with Hawk.

"Sure," Nikki replied. After telling the crew where she was going, she grabbed her jacket. Hawk helped her put it on and they walked outside into the brisk air. They crossed the street and walked along a path in the park. There weren't too many people there that afternoon.

"I hope it's a little warmer next week," Nikki said, cuddling close to Hawk as the air whipped through the park.

"It's supposed to be beautiful," Hawk said reassuringly. "Besides, it doesn't matter what the weather is like. I just want to be with you." He leaned down and kissed Nikki. They continued walking through the park. The leaves had turned brilliant shades of orange, red, and yellow. The wind had stopped for a moment, and Nikki reached down and picked up a yellow maple leaf. The leaf was perfect, and Nikki smiled. She twirled it around and watched it fall back to the ground.

"I should decorate my shop with these leaves," Nikki said.

"Great idea," Hawk said. Nikki made a mental note to come back out later with a bag to gather some leaves. After a little while she and Hawk turned back to the store. Nikki was about to walk across the street when Hawk stopped her.

"Have I told you lately how beautiful you are?" Hawk asked as he pulled Nikki close.

Nikki smiled. Hawk kissed her deeply, taking her breath away. She held Hawk close for a moment and then broke away.

"I have to get back to the shop," Nikki said, smiling.

"You could just call off of work. You are the owner, after all," Hawk said. Nikki laughed.

"I need to keep working on the wedding plans," Nikki said. Hawk smiled and walked her across the street. Nikki gave him a quick kiss and walked into the shop. There were a few new customers, and Nikki pulled off her jacket and helped them out. After the customers left, Nikki pulled out her cake plans.

"Now, here is what I was thinking for the top," Nikki said and started sketching again while Lidia, Tori, and Seth looked on. Lidia oohed and aahed while Seth smiled.

"Are you sure you'll be able to get that done in time?" Lidia asked.

"Positive," Nikki replied. "Hawk surprised me with the engagement. The least I can do is surprise him with this cake."

Lidia, Tori, and Seth looked on as Nikki drew out the final plans for the most intricate cake she'd ever made. Nikki knew she could create the cake in time for the wedding, she just needed to make sure her design was perfect. Just as she finished sketching, another customer walked in. Nikki put aside her sketch pad and helped the customer. Afterward, Tori and Seth went to lunch, and Nikki and Lidia took care of the chocolate shop.

chapter two

That evening, Hawk stopped by as Nikki was getting ready to close the shop. Seth and Tori had gone to a movie, and Nikki had allowed Lidia to leave early. There was one customer in the shop when Hawk arrived, and Nikki was helping her pick out some chocolates.

"I love cream-filled chocolates," the woman told Nikki. "Do you have any of those?"

"Yes, we have a nice selection of those," Nikki replied. "I have raspberry cream, lemon cream, and cherry cream."

"Those all sound delicious. Can I have half a pound of them mixed?" the woman asked Nikki.

"Of course," Nikki said. She picked out the chocolates and put them in a box. Nikki rang up the customer and bagged the box for her.

"Thank you," the customer said. "I live in the next town over. My friends told me I had to try out your award-winning chocolates. They look delicious."

Nikki thanked the customer. The woman smiled at Hawk as she left.

"Your reputation is growing," Hawk said. "You might have to put that award in a more prominent position." Nikki took her apron off and threw it at Hawk. He caught it and laughed.

"I thought we could head over to the diner for a bite to eat," Hawk said. "Seth told me he was taking Tori to the movies, so I knew you would be by yourself for dinner."

"Sure, just help me clean up," Nikki said. Hawk helped Nikki put away the chocolates and wipe down the counter and the tables. Nikki cleaned up the hot chocolate machine. While she counted her register, Hawk mopped the floor. Nikki thanked him.

"I have to drop this deposit off at the bank and then we can eat," Nikki said. "It's nice to have my own security detail," she joked, and Hawk laughed as he turned off the lights. It was already getting dark and Nikki was happy to have Hawk along. They walked to the bank where Nikki dropped off her deposit in the nighttime deposit chute. Hawk took her hand, and they strolled to the diner. The owner of the diner waved them to a booth, and they sat down. Their waitress appeared and took their order. She returned shortly with steaming hot coffees.

"Your food will be ready in a few minutes," she told Nikki and Hawk. Hawk thanked her and Nikki sipped her coffee.

"Is your tuxedo ready?" Nikki asked Hawk. Nikki had told Hawk that he could just wear a suit, but Hawk had insisted on wearing a tuxedo.

"It's hanging at my house, pressed and ready to go," Hawk said.

"And you coordinated the chairs at the gazebo?" Nikki asked.

"Yep. We will set them up first thing that morning," Hawk replied.

"That sounds great," Nikki said. It had been Hawk's idea to have the wedding in the park, and Nikki was glad she had agreed. The foliage made a beautiful backdrop to the gazebo.

"Just remember, as long as we are happy, nothing else matters," Nikki said. Honestly, Nikki would have been happy with a justice of the peace wedding, but Seth and Hawk had talked her out of that. Nikki realized it didn't matter where they were getting married. All that mattered was that they were happy. Hawk agreed.

"If you wanted to, I would get married right now in this diner," Hawk said.

Nikki laughed. "I don't think I'm dressed appropriately," Nikki said, looking down at her jeans and sweater.

"You look beautiful no matter what you wear," Hawk told her. Nikki leaned on his shoulder and Hawk put his arm around her.

Just then the food arrived. While Nikki and Hawk ate, they discussed the wedding more.

"Has Seth told you anything about the reception?" Nikki asked Hawk.

"Not a thing. They want to surprise us. All I know is that we have to show up at the mayor's house after the wedding," Hawk replied. Nikki sighed with contentment. She was glad Seth and Hawk got along so well. Hawk had taken Seth under his wing and had gotten him a job at the police department. Seth had passed the academy with flying colors and was now a rookie cop. Nikki was proud of him. She was also glad that he and Tori had taken over the reception. Nikki had just wanted a simple wedding, but Seth had insisted that other people would want to be included in the celebration. They compromised with a reception that Seth and Tori were planning. Lidia was assisting them, and that made Nikki happy.

Nikki turned to Hawk. "There is time to elope, you know," she said with a grin.

"Seth would shoot me," Hawk said, and they both laughed.

"Lidia would have my head on a plate," Nikki said. Hawk agreed, and they laughed again.

"It was very nice of the chief to offer to walk me down the aisle," Nikki said.

"He insisted," Hawk replied.

"I don't have any immediate family other than Seth, so I am glad for the family I have here," Nikki said. "It made picking out my maid of honor a piece of cake." Nikki smiled, remembering how excited Lidia was. Nikki was concerned that Tori would feel left out, but Tori said she would be busy with the reception, so everything was okay. It thrilled Nikki.

"Yep. Seth was happy to be my best man," Hawk replied. "I think some guys at the station are helping Tori and him with the reception."

"I just hope they let Tori do the decorating," Nikki laughed.

"They will," Hawk said, grinning. They both sat quietly for a moment.

"This is really happening, isn't it?" Nikki said.

"Yes ma'am," Hawk replied. He kissed Nikki and they finished their coffee. The waitress brought them two pieces of apple pie for dessert.

"Oh, we didn't order dessert," Nikki said.

"I was told to give it to the lovebirds," the waitress replied, smirking a little.

"Who told you that?" Hawk asked, looking around the diner.

"The gentleman at the table over there," the waitress pointed. Nikki and Hawk turned around. It was the chief.

"Hey, Dad, you should have joined us," Hawk called over to him. The chief rose from his chair and walked over.

"I already ate," the chief replied. "You two just enjoy your pie." He waved goodbye, and Hawk and Nikki dug into the sweet dessert. Hawk paid the bill after they finished. Hawk walked Nikki back to the chocolate shop.

"I would ask you to come over tonight, but I have some candies to make," Nikki said.

"That's okay. I have some paperwork to do. If I don't get it done tonight, I will hear about it tomorrow," Hawk replied, rolling his eyes.

Nikki knew that paperwork was one of Hawk's least favorite things. He would do anything if he could get out of doing paperwork. Nikki knew this report must be a week old if the chief was on Hawk's back.

"You need to get that done," Nikki said. "I'll be fine here by myself. I'll call you if I need you."

"Okay," Hawk agreed. "And call me when you get home."

"I will," Nikki promised. Hawk kissed her goodbye and Nikki let herself into the shop. She picked up her sketch pad and went into the kitchen. Nikki scanned her shelves and made a list of things she would need to buy for the cake. She paper-clipped that to the sketch pad and then went to work on making more chocolates for the shop. She made more maple leaves, some raspberry truffles, and some chocolate-covered crackers. Nikki could have kept going, but there was no more room in her refrigerator. She cleaned up the kitchen and grabbed her sketch pad.

Since Hawk had paperwork to do, Nikki could go to the grocery store alone. She was glad for the opportunity since she was shopping for the ingredients for the wedding cake. One reason she won the chocolate competition was because the judges liked the flavor of her chocolates. She didn't use too many fancy ingredients like her competitors had. Some of her competitors thought her chocolates were too simple. She had shown them all and took home the prize. Nikki smiled, remembering the competition. She grabbed the things she needed for the wedding cake and checked out. After taking the ingredients back to the chocolate shop, she drove home. She called Hawk to let him know she made it home okay, and after they chatted for a few minutes, she hung up. She relaxed in a hot bath and made herself some hot cocoa afterward.

"I hope Hawk is right about the weather," Nikki said aloud. "If it doesn't warm up, I will walk down the aisle in a sweater." Nikki laughed to herself as she crawled into bed with a book. She read until she heard Seth come in and then she turned out her light and went to sleep.

chapter three

The next morning Nikki woke up and smelled coffee brewing. She looked at her clock and realized her alarm had not gone off yet. *I wonder why Seth is up so early,* Nikki thought as she put on her robe. Nikki walked by Seth's room. The door was closed, and she thought she heard a light snore. Nikki stopped and turned back toward her room. If Seth had not made the coffee, who had? She was about to go back to her bedroom when someone cleared their throat. Nikki turned around and saw Hawk at the bottom of the stairs.

"You scared me to death," Nikki chastised Hawk in a loud whisper. Hawk smiled and went back into the kitchen. Nikki followed him with a grin. Hawk had not only brewed coffee, he had also made pancakes and eggs. Hawk told Nikki to sit down and gave her a cup of coffee. Nikki thanked him and watched as Hawk maneuvered around her kitchen. Nikki's kitchen was on the smaller side, but Hawk managed to make and serve breakfast without elbowing her or knocking any platters off the counters. Hawk put a plate of pancakes, eggs, and bacon in front of Nikki.

"Eat up," Hawk said.

"Thank you," Nikki replied. She waited until Hawk had

his plate and had sat down across from her and then they both enjoyed their breakfast.

"So, what is the special occasion?" Nikki asked. "You don't normally show up and cook me breakfast."

"I wanted to surprise you," Hawk said. "You have been working overtime planning this wedding and I thought you could use a bit of a break."

"I appreciate that," Nikki replied and sipped her coffee. They heard a thunk, and Nikki and Hawk looked at each other. There were two other thunks, and Seth appeared. He was wearing his uniform and had run down the stairs.

"What time is it?" Seth asked as he bounded into the kitchen.

"Slow down," Nikki said. "It's still early."

"Whew, that's a relief. I smelled the coffee and thought I was running late. Oh, hi, Hawk," Seth said as he noticed Hawk sitting across from Nikki.

"Seth has been getting up before me and brewing the coffee," Nikki explained to Hawk as Seth helped himself to some breakfast. Hawk laughed.

"It is better to be a little early to work," Hawk told Seth.

"I agree," Seth replied, sitting down beside Nikki. They all relaxed and enjoyed the home-cooked meal. Afterward, Seth and Hawk cleaned up while Nikki took a shower and got ready for work. When Nikki went back downstairs, Seth was putting on his coat.

"I'm off to work, Mom," Seth said.

"Have fun and be safe," Nikki replied. Seth left and Nikki went back into the kitchen. Hawk was drying the dishes and Nikki walked up behind him. She put her arms around him and rested her head on his back. Hawk put down the dish and turned around. He hugged Nikki close and kissed her. Just then Hawk's radio went off. It was a call about a home break-in just outside of town. Nikki sighed as Hawk threw on his jacket. Hawk kissed her goodbye and ran out the door. Nikki finished putting the dishes away and put on her jacket.

"It's time to make the chocolates," Nikki said to herself as she walked out to her car. She drove the short distance into town and opened up her shop. Tori and Lidia appeared shortly afterward and helped Nikki set up the chocolate display. Tori opened the register and Nikki went back into the kitchen.

Nikki organized the chocolate ingredients for the icing and decorations on the cake. She was planning to create some decorations that afternoon. Nikki heard her door chime and she peeked out into the store. A mother and her toddler son had appeared. Lidia was helping the woman, and Tori was distracting the child. Nikki smiled. Tori would make a wonderful mother someday. Nikki turned back to her kitchen. She finished organizing the ingredients and thought about the cake itself.

Nikki had been making cakes all summer for parties, picnics, weddings, and other occasions. She had used those opportunities to see exactly what kind of cake Hawk liked. For one party Nikki had made a strawberry sponge cake. Hawk liked it, but he said the sponge was a little dry for his taste. For a birthday party Nikki had made a vanilla cake with chocolate frosting. Hawk liked that more. For one of the weddings, Nikki had created a marble cake with white chocolate frosting. Hawk had really liked that cake but thought the frosting was too sweet, so Nikki made a marble cake with regular chocolate frosting. Nikki looked at her list to be sure she had all the ingredients and realized she still had a few things to buy.

When Nikki stepped back into the store, there was a small line at the counter, so Nikki helped Lidia and Tori with the customers. After a few minutes everyone had been taken care of. Nikki told Lidia and Tori that she was going to the store to get a few more ingredients for the wedding cake.

"Go on. We'll be fine while you are gone," Lidia said.

"Thank you," Nikki replied as she walked out the door. The wind had died down, and the sun was trying to shine through the clouds overhead. Nikki drove to the store past the overgrown maple and evergreen forests. She got to the store, parked, and walked in. Nikki walked down the baking aisle. A woman from town was there and Nikki said hello.

"Are you shopping for your latest chocolate creation?" the woman asked Nikki.

"No," Nikki replied, laughing. "I am shopping for a surprise for Hawk."

"Oh, how wonderful," the woman exclaimed. "I'm sure he will love whatever you cook up." Nikki thanked her and the woman moved on. Nikki grabbed some vanilla beans, dark and light chocolate, and cinnamon. Nikki picked up a few more things she needed and checked out. Then she drove back to the chocolate store down the windy roads and parked her car. She carried her bags inside the shop and deposited them on the kitchen table. Nikki took off her jacket and checked the front of the store. There were quite a few customers, so Nikki pitched in and helped Tori and Lidia. After the wave of customers had been taken care of, Nikki and Tori restocked the shelves. A little while later the door opened, and Seth appeared. He said hello to Nikki and Lidia and gave Tori a hug and a kiss.

"What are you doing here?" Nikki asked. It was not lunch time yet, and Seth had his uniform on.

"I have a couple of minutes and I thought I would swing by and see what everyone was up to," Seth said.

Nikki smiled. "Where is your partner?" she asked.

"He is at the precinct doing paperwork. I finished mine so he told me to take a break," Seth replied. Nikki laughed. Hawk was mentoring Seth but was not his partner. Seth's partner had been on the force for a while. He hated paperwork as much as Hawk did and dragged his feet about processing it. Seth probably had a good half hour to kill.

"So, I've bought all the ingredients for the wedding cake," Nikki said.

"What did you get?" Tori asked.

"I will make a marble cake, but I have to decide what kind of chocolate I am going to use," Nikki replied.

"You should use white chocolate," Tori said. "That way the chocolate taste will be a surprise."

"I had not thought about that," Nikki said. "I think the white chocolate will be a little too sweet for Hawk, but I will definitely use that idea for a future cake." Tori beamed.

"Milk chocolate is not as sweet as white chocolate. How about using a milk chocolate cake batter?" Lidia asked.

"I thought about that, but I was not sure if the vanilla would overpower the milk chocolate. I will be using fresh vanilla beans and they can be strong," Nikki said.

"Seems like dark chocolate is your only option then," Seth said. "That should balance with the vanilla flavor."

"That is what I will probably use," Nikki said. Just then Seth's radio squawked. Nikki could not understand what the call was, but Seth went flying out the door.

"Be safe," chorused Nikki, Lidia, and Tori.

A few customers appeared and Nikki helped them with their chocolate choices. Lidia cleaned off the tables and Tori made more hot chocolate. The store grew busy and Nikki had to put off making her cake to assist her customers. The day went on and Seth did not return. Tori and Lidia went to lunch and Nikki watched the store. Nikki was happy that her chocolate shop was busy, but she was concerned about getting the cake made. Nikki decided she would just stay after work that evening and get it done then. Lidia and Tori reappeared with a turkey sandwich and some hot tea for Nikki. She thanked them and went back into the kitchen to eat. That afternoon Nikki made more chocolates and designed a new truffle. She walked back into her shop and it was quiet.

"It finally died down," Tori said. "Not that I am complaining." Nikki laughed.

"Hey, have you heard from Seth?" Nikki asked Tori.

"No. I figured he was too busy for lunch," Tori replied.

"You are probably right," Nikki said, and she grabbed a cloth to wipe the tables again. Lidia fixed some more hot chocolate and Tori restocked the candies.

"We will probably need to make more chocolates for tomorrow," Tori told Nikki. "There are only a few sheets left in the refrigerator."

"I just made a couple of batches a while ago," Nikki replied.

"Yep, and they are going in the case now," Tori said. Nikki was happy that her chocolates were selling.

"If you and Lidia can watch the shop, I will make more," Nikki said. Tori agreed and Nikki went back to the kitchen.

chapter four

Nikki put on her apron and got out the ingredients for some chocolate-covered pretzels. She also pulled out the ingredients for caramel. Nikki liked to dip the pretzels in caramel and then in the chocolate. This gave them an extra layer of goodness and her customers loved them. After Nikki made the caramel, she heated up the dark chocolate. She dipped the pretzels into the caramel and then the chocolate and put them on a pan. She put the pan in the refrigerator to cool down. Nikki then made some drop milk chocolates with some drizzled salted caramel on top. Nikki also made delicate caramel balls by dripping the caramel to highlight the case. She stuck these into the refrigerator as well.

Nikki then pulled out the ingredients for truffles. Nikki was hands deep in chocolate in her kitchen. She had decided to make some more truffles and she was rolling them in her milk chocolate dust. Nikki placed them on a sheet and when the sheet was full, she put it into the refrigerator. Nikki was happy with her truffle recipe. She was planning to make a fall assortment of truffles after the wedding. She would use white chocolate with orange, yellow, and red food dye. The orange ones would have an orange flavor, the yellow ones would be lemon flavored, and the red would be raspberry. Nikki had thought about putting some jam inside them instead of the flavoring. Nikki made a note to try some out and see what worked the best.

After making the truffles, Nikki cleaned up and contemplated what she would do next. All of the cases in the front were full of candies and right now they were selling without any tweaks. Nikki was happy she could make what she wanted without worrying about what the customers thought. Nikki stood by the sink and thought she might get started on the cake for her wedding. She pulled out the pots and pans she would need along with the ingredients. Just as she was about to crack the first egg, her cell phone rang. It was Seth.

"Mom, can you come out to the cabins?" Seth asked Nikki.

"I was just starting to work on the cake," Nikki replied.

"We need you out here right away," Seth replied. "It's urgent." Nikki caught his serious tone and told him to text her the address. Nikki raced out into the front of the store and told Lidia and Tori about Seth's call.

"I am not sure what the emergency is," Nikki said. "I just hope Hawk is okay."

"Go ahead and meet up with Seth," Tori replied. "I'll take care of closing the shop." Nikki mentioned the cake and Tori said she would clean up the kitchen. Nikki thanked her and ran out the door to her car, pausing to check her phone. She saw the message from Seth and pulled up the address. Outside of town there were some hunting cabins. Nikki knew the approximate location of the cabins, but she needed the address to get to the exact location where Seth was waiting for her. Nikki drove out of town and along some back roads. There were dense trees on either side of the winding roads, with no apparent streets or turn-offs. Nikki went up a long hill and slowed down. Nikki turned off into what appeared to be some grass in between two trees but was really a trail to a cabin in the woods. Nikki drove along the bumpy trail until it got too dense. Nikki got out of her car and ran down the trail the rest of the way to the cabin. Seth met her along the way.

"Is Hawk okay?" Nikki asked with concern.

"Yes, he's fine," Seth replied. "Come with me." Seth led her around a large stone by the trail to the front of the cabin. Nikki saw Hawk and jogged up to him, noticing how pale he appeared. Nikki looked down at the ground. A man with a fishing vest and a fishing hat on his head was lying face up on the ground. There was what looked like a gunshot wound in his chest and he appeared dead.

Suddenly Nikki gasped. "Is that Luke?" she asked.

"Yes, it is," Hawk replied. Nikki turned and gave Hawk a hug. Luke was a police officer who had been on the force for a long time. Hawk had known Luke for most of his life. Luke was a dear friend of Hawk's father.

"I am so sorry, Hawk," Nikki said. She let go of Hawk and looked at Luke. It was apparent Luke had been dead for a little while. Nikki looked at the gunshot wound and noticed something on Luke's fishing vest.

"What is this?" Nikki asked as she stooped closer. Hawk knelt down beside Nikki. There was a small note pinned to Luke's fishing vest. Nikki used a gloved hand to remove the note. She and Hawk stood up. Nikki read the note aloud.

"I am coming for the chief next," Nikki read out loud. "Oh no, what is happening, Hawk?"

"I don't know, but we will find out," Hawk replied. Just then they heard a voice speaking loudly nearby.

"Let me through, I am your chief," Nikki heard. She turned around and saw Seth blocking the chief's path. Hawk moved quickly and stood beside Seth.

"You do not want to go over there, Dad," Hawk said. "I'm so sorry. It's Luke."

"What's wrong? I came up here to meet him for some

fishing and I saw all of your cars here. I didn't hear this being called on the radio," the chief replied.

"I told the guys to keep radio silence about this until I could talk to you myself," Hawk replied.

"What's wrong with Luke?" Chief asked. Hawk looked away, unable to respond, and Nikki spoke.

"I am sorry, Chief, but Luke is dead," Nikki said. Hawk steadied his father as he received the news.

"What happened?" the chief asked.

"He was shot," Hawk replied.

"There was a note pinned to his fishing vest," Nikki told the chief. "The text was threatening to you."

"Let me see the note and Luke," the chief insisted. Nikki showed him the note. The chief read it through the evidence bag.

"I think we should get you somewhere safe," Hawk told his father.

"I am not going anywhere," the chief replied. "I want to investigate the scene."

Nikki knew the chief would not budge so she wasn't surprised when Hawk stepped aside to let his father through to the crime scene. The chief walked over to Luke's body and took his hat off. He knelt down and closed Luke's eyes. The chief stood up and carefully examined the body. The chief looked upset, but he carefully studied the location and Luke. Forensics appeared and they started to gather information.

"We should probably let them have the scene," Hawk told his father. "I can call the office and find a place for you to stay where it is safe." The chief scowled and walked off. Hawk started to follow him, but Nikki put her hand on Hawk's arm and stopped him.

"Let me talk to him," Nikki said. Hawk reluctantly agreed, and Nikki walked over to the pond where the chief was standing.

chapter five

Nikki followed the chief to the large pond, which was surrounded by a densely grown forest. The chief liked to come out here to hunt and fish. He owned another larger cabin where Hawk had taken Nikki after he proposed to her. The chief was standing looking over the water. The water was still and reflected the trees surrounding it. Nikki could see the pain of his loss in the lines on his face. They stood silently side by side for a while contemplating the scenery. Nikki realized the chief was also scouring the woods for any clues. She watched him look carefully and precisely over the water. Nikki knew the chief did not want to be excluded from the investigation, and putting him under protection would hamper his ability to help Hawk with the case.

"You know, Hawk is just looking out for you. Having you in protective custody will keep you safe while the others work the case," Nikki said to the chief after a while.

"I understand," he replied. "Do you know what it is like to be in protective custody?"

Nikki shook her head. She had an idea, but it had never been fully explained to her. Her ex-husband had been relocated but he was not in protective custody.

"You cannot go anywhere or talk to anyone," the chief explained. "You have to be cautious and avoid windows and doors. You will usually end up in some run-down motel because it is easier and cheaper to keep an eye on you. Luke's death is my fault, and I need to be the one who helps solve his murder. I cannot do that in protective custody." Nikki understood but she let the chief keep talking.

"I invited Luke to the cabin. I was supposed to meet him here a couple of hours ago, but I was running late. If I had been here, he might still be alive. We were supposed to go fishing and have a relaxing weekend. I got hung up in town helping Mrs. Smith with her damaged mailbox. It turned out that Mr. Smith had backed into it. I should have let someone else handle her complaint, but she asked for me personally. If I had only been here…"

"If you had been here you might be the one lying on the ground," a male voice said behind them. Nikki jumped a little and turned around. It was Hawk.

"You need to stop startling me," Nikki scolded Hawk.

"Did you find out the time of death?" Hawk's father asked.

"Forensics estimates that he died about a couple of hours ago. You would have been here when the killer was here. I am sorry Luke is dead, but I am happy you are still here," Hawk replied. The chief looked at his son and sighed.

"He blames himself for Luke's death," Nikki told Hawk. "That is a heavy burden to be carrying."

"I understand, Dad," Hawk said, putting his hand on his dad's shoulder. "I still would feel better with you in protective custody."

"I want to assist you on the case," the chief insisted. "Nikki will not be able to help you, she has a wedding to plan."

Nikki looked up, startled. "Oh, don't worry about that. I am helping Hawk with this case," she replied earnestly. "No one threatens you while I am around." The chief gave Nikki a small smile.

"But your wedding. I want you to have the best day possible. How can you plan things and investigate this case?" Chief asked Nikki.

"The wedding is not as important as your safety. Your life comes first, so we will figure this out," Nikki replied. "Besides, I have people who are willing to help with the wedding plans. I will put more on them. How can I have a wedding if your life is in danger?"

"There is not going to be a wedding?" someone asked behind Hawk. Hawk moved aside and Nikki saw Seth.

"We may have to postpone the wedding until the killer is in custody. I don't want to take any chances," Nikki explained.

"Oh, okay," Seth said. "Hawk, forensics is almost done. They asked if you could meet them back at the station."

"Sure," Hawk replied. "Let them know I will be there as soon as I convince my father to go into protective custody."

"Hold on, Seth," Nikki said, as Seth turned to go. "Hawk, I have an idea that just might work."

"I'm listening," Hawk said.

"What if the chief comes to my house? It is secluded and you can position men around the perimeter. Chief can stay there and still assist us with the case. Win-win."

"I don't know." Hawk looked uncertain.

"With the money you will be saving on motel costs, you can pay the officers overtime to watch the house," Nikki replied.

"It's a good plan," Hawk said, "except I don't like putting you at risk. Someone is trying to kill my father. I am not happy that he will be staying at my fiancé's house."

"It's not like I can't take care of myself," Nikki replied.

"I like this idea. That way I can still help with the case," the chief said to Nikki.

"I don't want you working on this case. It's too dangerous," Hawk told his father.

"I will stay at Nikki's and work through the evidence you collect. I can use her computer and stay in the loop," the chief replied.

"I want someone with you at all times," Hawk said. "Not just outside Nikki's house."

"I can do that," Seth said. Nikki and Hawk both balked.

"It is too dangerous," Nikki said.

"You just started on the force," Hawk added. "I will not put you at risk."

"I'll be okay. I have been through training and I am ready to step up," Seth said.

"I think he is ready," the chief said. "Besides, he knows the house and the surrounding area better than anyone else on the force."

"That is true," Nikki conceded.

"Okay," Hawk agreed reluctantly. "I want two officers at the house with you at all times."

"Agreed," the chief said.

"Well then, it's settled. Seth, tell forensics Hawk will be there soon. You and Chief ride back to my place. I will follow behind and get everyone settled in," Nikki said.

"Okay, but I will be staying there at night as extra security," Hawk said.

"I have no objections to that," Nikki said with a grin. Hawk actually grinned back. Nikki was glad to see that. She was worried that Hawk would stress himself out. Hawk left to go to his office. Seth and the chief took off for Nikki's house, and Nikki went back to the shop to make sure everything was closed up. The shop was closed and locked, so Nikki drove home.

Seth and the chief were there. Seth offered to put the chief in his bedroom. Nikki thanked him and changed the sheets and made the room comfortable for the chief. Meanwhile,

Tori stopped by with some food from the diner. Seth had told her what was going on. Nikki thanked her for the food and for closing the shop. Hawk appeared and they all sat down to eat. After dinner, Tori left and the chief and Seth went into the front room to watch television. Hawk helped Nikki clean up the kitchen.

"I'm not sure where you are going to sleep tonight. The chief is in Seth's room. Seth was going to take the couch, but I'll ask him to let you have it," Nikki said.

"No, don't do that. I can take the floor," Hawk responded. Nikki smiled. He was such a gentleman. They finished the dishes and joined the others in the front room.

"I think I am going to head upstairs to bed," the chief said.

"I am going to do a perimeter walk and make sure the deputies are at their assigned posts," Hawk replied.

"I can go with you," Seth told Hawk.

"Why don't you stay here in case there is any trouble?" Hawk replied. Seth agreed and Nikki put him to work setting up the sofa and blowing up an air mattress. Hawk came back and Nikki kissed him goodnight. She went upstairs and got ready for bed. Sleep did not come easy that night as every noise outside made Nikki jump. After a couple of hours, she finally drifted off and slept undisturbed until morning.

chapter six

The next morning Nikki woke up and smelled coffee brewing. *I could get used to this,* Nikki thought and then laughed, realizing this would be her life very soon, but without all the police presence. She got up and took a quick shower, then got dressed and went downstairs. Seth, Hawk, the chief, and Tori were all in the kitchen. Seth was pouring coffee and Hawk was making breakfast.

"Good morning, handsome," Nikki whispered into Hawk's ear as she gave him a quick hug. Hawk smiled and kissed her good morning.

"Good morning, Nikki," the chief said.

"Good morning, Chief, everyone," Nikki replied. She sat down at the table and Seth poured her some coffee. Hawk dished out breakfast for everyone and sat down next to Nikki. The chief was at the head of the table and Tori and Seth were across from Nikki and Hawk.

"So, what are the plans for today?" Nikki asked Hawk.

"Well, I am waiting to hear from forensics," Hawk replied. "I thought I would dig into some of Dad's old cases and see if there were any clues there."

"Good idea," the chief said.

"Don't worry about the shop," Tori told Nikki. "Lidia and

I talked yesterday. We can handle the store while you help Hawk. You need to find out who killed Luke."

"Thank you," Nikki replied. "Okay, that takes care of the store. I can come in with you and sort through some files."

"Excellent," Hawk replied. "I always enjoy having you around to help out."

"As long as the wedding is being planned, I am fine with whatever you do," the chief said. Nikki smiled. Everyone enjoyed their breakfast. The chief offered to clean up the kitchen.

"Since I am not allowed to leave," he sighed.

Hawk laughed. "Try and relax, Dad. I will email you some files to look through," Hawk told the chief.

Hawk left for his office and Tori left to open the chocolate shop. Nikki stayed back to make sure Seth and the chief had everything they needed.

"I have some lunch meat in the refrigerator if you want some," Nikki said. "There is plenty of tea and lemonade."

"Thank you," said the chief. "We will be fine."

Nikki put her jacket on and left the house. She said goodbye to the deputy near the door and drove into town. She circled by the chocolate shop and was happy to see it lit up and ready to go. She then drove over to the station. She went inside and found Hawk with a pile of folders by his desk.

"You know they digitized these last month," Nikki said. Hawk looked up and rolled his eyes.

"I prefer paper," he replied. Nikki laughed and sat down across from Hawk. They sorted through files for a couple of hours until Hawk stood up and stretched. They had not found anything helpful yet.

"I am going to get some coffee. Would you like some?" Hawk asked Nikki.

"Yes, please," Nikki said. She stood up and walked around a little bit and then stretched. She sat back down and checked her phone, texting Tori to see how the shop was running. Tori responded quickly and told her everything was fine. Hawk reappeared with the coffee. Nikki thanked him and he sat down.

"We need to solve this quickly," Nikki said to Hawk.

"I agree," Hawk said, sipping his coffee.

"I would hate to have to postpone the wedding," Nikki said.

"That should not happen," Hawk said. "But if it does, it is okay. I love you and want to be married to you. I can wait a little longer if I have to." Nikki smiled and put down her cup. She reached over the desk and gave Hawk a hug and kiss.

"I love you," Nikki said to Hawk.

"I love you too," Hawk replied, kissing her again.

"Okay, let's get back to these files," Nikki said. She sat down and opened the next file on the large pile beside her. Hawk lifted his next file and opened it and started to read.

After a few hours Hawk told Nikki he was hungry. Nikki agreed she could use some lunch and some fresh air. The forensic team had not called Hawk, so they went over to the lab to see if the technicians had found anything. The tech on duty told Hawk they did not have any clues yet besides the note. Hawk was disappointed but the tech said they were trying to match an incomplete fingerprint they pulled from the note.

"It is not much, but it might be a clue," the technician said. Hawk thanked him. Nikki wanted to stop by the store to see how Lidia and Tori were managing. They entered the chocolate shop and Tori and Lidia greeted them. There were no customers at the moment, but Tori said it had been a busy morning.

"Do you need us to eat here so you can get a break?" Nikki asked Tori.

"Nope, we ordered pizza delivery. It should be here soon," Tori replied.

"Okay," Nikki said. Tori and Lidia reassured her that they had the store handled.

"I will make the deposit tonight and bring by the receipt later," Tori told Nikki. Nikki thanked her. Tori was growing into a great store manager. Nikki was glad she and Seth were together. It was nice to have someone around to help Lidia in the chocolate shop when Nikki couldn't be there. Nikki thanked Lidia and Tori and she and Hawk left.

"Pizza sounds good," Hawk said.

"We can split a small pizza and take it back to the office and eat while we sort through the files," Nikki offered.

"That is a great idea," Hawk replied. They went to the pizza shop and got a small pepperoni pizza and drinks to go. As they were leaving, Nikki glanced over toward the park and wondered if she would be getting married soon. Nikki shook her head and got into the car with Hawk.

Hawk seemed to know what Nikki was thinking. "We will be married on time," he declared. Nikki squeezed his hand and wished she had half of Hawk's confidence when it came to their wedding. They drove back to Hawk's office and sorted through files for the rest of the day. The day dragged on, and Nikki and Hawk still did not have any leads by dinnertime.

Nikki and Hawk drove to Nikki's house after work. Nikki made dinner and Hawk talked to the chief and Seth. Tori appeared in the kitchen.

"How are you holding up?" Tori asked Nikki.

"I'm okay," Nikki replied. "There is just so much to do before our wedding. I haven't even made the cake yet. Maybe we should postpone."

"Whatever you decide to do, Lidia and I will support

you," Tori replied. Nikki gave her a quick hug and thanked her. "Let me set the table while you finish dinner," Tori told Nikki.

Later, when everyone was around the table, Nikki mentioned postponing the wedding.

"We can put it off for a week. That won't make much of a difference," Nikki said.

"Absolutely not," the chief said. "I will not be the reason you two are not married. If I have to stay put here while you are at the wedding, you will be married on the day you are scheduled to be. If you need help with getting things together, I have all the time in the world. Hawk, give me your list. I can take care of anything I can from the house."

"You are not supposed to make any calls," Hawk reminded him.

"I'm not, but he can," said the chief, pointing to Seth. Everyone laughed, and Hawk agreed that Seth could help him with his wedding chores. Seth said he was happy to help. Nikki was still worried about the cake, but she didn't mention it out loud. She wanted it to be a surprise for Hawk.

After dinner Seth and Tori did the dishes while everyone else watched television in the living room. Nikki sat on the sofa holding Hawk's hand while the chief sat in a loveseat away from the front window. All the curtains were drawn in the house. Hawk had installed some extra security cameras for added protection. Nikki had taken the deputies on duty some food and coffee. After the news was over, Hawk checked the security feeds from the cameras. They were all clear. The chief and Seth monitored them during the day and the deputies on duty took over at night. Nikki made some hot chocolate for everyone and they sat and watched a movie. When the movie was over, Tori left and Hawk walked the perimeter. It was late by then, so everyone decided to go to sleep. Nikki tossed and turned all night and the next morning woke up reluctantly.

chapter seven

The next morning Nikki told Hawk she wanted to work in the store for an hour. Hawk agreed, so Nikki drove over after breakfast. Lidia and Tori were surprised to see her.

"I had to get away from the files for a little while," Nikki told them. "I just want to spend some time in the kitchen. Are there any candies that I need to make?" Tori told Nikki that they were almost out of truffles. Tori offered to make them, but Nikki declined. She just wanted to be alone in the kitchen for a little while. She shut the door and sat down. Nikki had not slept well the night before, so she let her mind wander for a little bit.

Nikki was not feeling festive or excited at all. She wondered why she was so down. It was not just the stress of planning the wedding and getting the cake made. It wasn't even the investigation into Luke's murder. Nikki admitted to herself that she was having doubts. She did not doubt that she wanted to marry Hawk. That was certain. Nikki was just concerned that they were running into marriage too quickly. Nikki got married the first time at a justice of the peace when she was pregnant with Seth. That marriage did not end well. Nikki had known her previous husband for only a few months before they got married. It was a quick decision and a quick ceremony. Nikki admitted she never should have married him. At least Nikki had gotten away and moved with Seth to Maple Hills. She loved living here and she loved Hawk. She just was not sure if she should be rushing into this wedding.

There was a knock on the door and Nikki jumped. She realized she had been daydreaming for half an hour.

"Are you okay?" Lidia asked Nikki.

"I'm fine," Nikki replied. She cleared her head and started to work on the truffles. She pulled out the chocolate and proceeded to melt it with some confectioner's sugar and other ingredients. Nikki laid some parchment paper in a container and poured the chocolate mixture into the container and stuck it in the refrigerator. While the mixture was cooling, Nikki shaved some milk chocolate. She then mixed in some gold shavings with the milk chocolate.

While she was working on the truffles, Nikki had some ideas for the cake. She wrote down the ideas in her planner and felt a bit better about having things ready in time for the wedding. Nikki pulled out the chocolate mixture from the refrigerator and rolled her truffles. She put them back into the refrigerator to cool. Nikki then quickly made up some chocolate-covered pretzels and stuck them in the refrigerator. She went out front and helped Lidia and Tori with a few customers.

A young man in his twenties was standing by the counter looking at the chocolates. Nikki noticed he was frowning.

"May I help you?" Nikki asked.

"I am going to propose to my girlfriend tonight. I was hoping to give her some of your truffles, but I see that you are out. Do you have something else you would suggest?"

Nikki smiled. "I just got done making some special truffles. They are cooling right now. Can you come back in an hour? I will have them boxed and ready for you."

"Thank you so much." The young man beamed. "I thought some designer chocolates would go well with the engagement ring."

"Designer chocolates?" Nikki asked. Tori coughed nearby. Nikki turned to her.

"What do you know about designer chocolates?" Nikki asked Tori. Tori blushed a little.

"I may have added a hashtag to your social media," Tori said.

"What are you talking about?" Nikki asked.

"Here, I'll show you," the young man said. He pulled out his phone and showed Nikki her website. There was a section for hashtags and chocolates, homemade, Maple Hills, and others were already listed. Nikki looked closely. #designerchocolates was now on the list.

"It is a correct description," the young man said. "They are homemade and bumped up a few levels from regular homemade chocolates. And, since you won the chocolate contest, you have the credibility to stand behind that claim."

Nikki rolled her eyes. "Fine, it can stay on the webpage," Nikki said. "But next time, please run it by me before changing my website," Nikki told Tori. Tori agreed. The young man said he would be back for the truffles. When he left, Nikki told Tori she would have to arrange the truffles for the young man.

"And give him a gift card for the shop since I did not have the truffles here when he wanted them," Nikki added. "And wrap them in the deluxe gold gift wrap."

"Okay," Tori replied.

"I should be getting over to Hawk's office," Nikki said to Tori and Lidia. They each gave Nikki a hug and wished her well.

"I hope you find some leads soon," Lidia told Nikki.

"I do too," Nikki replied. She left the chocolate shop with two cups of coffee. Nikki shook her head and thought, *designer chocolates?* She put the coffees in the car cup holders and drove to Hawk's office. On the way, Nikki's mind wandered again. She thought about where they would live after they were married. Hawk's house was too small for them and Hawk did not want to move into Nikki's house. Nikki realized they would have to buy or rent a house. Somehow, this had not yet crossed Nikki's mind, and she gasped. She did not want to purchase another house. Nikki calmed herself down and figured they would work out the details about where they would live later. Suddenly she had an idea. She turned the car around and went back to the shop.

"I thought you were going to the station," Tori said.

"I was, but I just had an epiphany," Nikki replied, rushing into the kitchen. She pulled out her wedding notebook and scribbled out the design ideas. She started sketching and a few minutes later was very happy with the results. Tori came in to restock the shelves and wrap the truffles. She gasped.

"That is a beautiful idea. Are you sure you can make it?" Tori asked Nikki.

"Absolutely," Nikki said. "The best part is that I can use what I have here. I don't need to buy anything else. Now I just need to find the time to make it." Tori laughed. She pulled out the chocolate pretzels.

"The truffles need a few more minutes," she told Nikki. Nikki agreed.

"Can you take care of them and get that box ready if I go over to Hawk's office?" Nikki asked Tori.

"Yep," Tori replied. Nikki thanked her and left. The coffee was still warm as Nikki drove to the station. This time, she made it to Hawk's office.

"Here you go," Nikki said, handing Hawk a cup of coffee. Nikki could tell Hawk was stressed out. She went around the desk and put her hands on Hawk's shoulders. She rubbed his shoulders and he tilted his head back.

"That feels wonderful. Thank you," Hawk said. "And thank you for the coffee."

"Have you heard back from forensics?" Nikki asked.

"Not yet. They are still looking for anything that can help us," Hawk replied. Nikki stopped rubbing his shoulders and gave Hawk a quick kiss.

"Well, let's keep going through these files," Nikki said. Hawk sighed and Nikki sat down. She opened a file and looked through. This one was about a case where the chief had arrested a man for stealing some cars. The man had just gotten out on parole last week.

"How about him?" Nikki asked Hawk. Hawk looked at the file. He shook his head.

"This is Pete," Hawk said. "He now works for the police in their mechanics shop. Dad got him the job and he worked part time here while he was still in jail before he got paroled. He is now able to work full time for us. He loves my dad and is grateful to him for helping him go straight."

"That was nice of your father to get him that job," Nikki said. "I am not surprised, though. Your father is a nice man." Hawk smiled.

"That's part of the reason it's so hard to come up with leads. My dad might be gruff on the outside, but he is soft on the inside. If you prove yourself to him, he will have your back forever," Hawk said. Nikki nodded. She had learned that lesson. While the whole town was against her at one time, the chief had stood up for her and had her back. Nikki was grateful for the chief's kindness. She looked through some more files.

"Are these the last of them?" Nikki asked Hawk.

"Not nearly," Hawk replied. "We have several more boxes left." Nikki sighed. She did not give up, though. Nikki knew the chief would never give up when it came to her and she was not giving up when it came to finding Luke's killer.

Nikki looked through the rest of the files on her desk and pulled another box over.

"What is this blue folder?" Nikki asked Hawk. All of the other folders were plain manila folders. This was a blue plastic folder.

"I'm not sure. Maybe they ran out of regular folders," Hawk said.

Nikki opened the file. She gasped and started to laugh.

"What is it?" Hawk asked.

"Where did you get these files?" Nikki asked Hawk.

"From my dad's office," Hawk replied.

"Well, this one is different. It's not a case file," Nikki said.

"What is it?" Hawk asked.

"Come and see for yourself," Nikki said. Hawk walked over and groaned. The blue plastic file contained pictures of Hawk when he was younger. There were pictures of him fishing with his father and pictures of Hawk when he was a baby. Nikki turned and looked at Hawk. He was blushing.

"These are adorable," Nikki said. There were not too many pictures of Hawk as a child in the chief's house. Nikki had never asked about them, but she was happy to come across this treasure trove. Hawk picked up a picture. Nikki could see some tears at the corners of his eyes. Nikki stood up and looked at the picture. It was a picture of a beautiful woman holding Hawk on her lap. The chief was standing behind them in his uniform.

"Is that your mom?" Nikki asked Hawk.

"Yes," Hawk replied.

"She was beautiful," Nikki said.

"Yes, she was," Hawk agreed. He put the picture back into the folder. Nikki took the folder and put it in her purse.

"What are you doing with that?" Hawk asked.

"I want us to look through it at home," Nikki said. "I am sure there are some great stories that go along with these pictures."

"Okay," Hawk agreed. "Now can we get back to work?" Nikki laughed and grabbed the next folder. She and Hawk worked for another half hour.

"I might have something," Hawk said.

Nikki looked up. "What did you find?" she asked. Hawk showed her the folder and Nikki agreed it could be a lead. Hawk laid it to the side. Nikki and Hawk continued searching with a renewed vigor. Nikki found another folder that might be useful. Hawk found one more and they agreed that those were the most likely suspects. Hawk and Nikki had gone through all the files. Hawk grabbed the three files and they went to Nikki's house to fill in the chief.

chapter eight

Back at Nikki's house, Hawk showed the chief the files they found. The chief agreed that those were good suspects. One of them had killed someone, and, according to Hawk and the chief, the others were also capable of murder.

"How come that person is allowed to walk free?" Nikki asked about the person who had killed someone.

"He was a juvenile at the time. He served his time and was released recently," Hawk replied. "I am going to question all of the suspects tomorrow."

"I am going to go with you," Nikki said. The chief smiled.

"No, you are not," Hawk replied.

"What do you mean?" Nikki asked. "And do not tell me I have to make wedding plans, or I will call off the whole thing."

"That is not what I was going to say," Hawk replied. "I am just concerned because everyone on our list has served time. These are hardened criminals. I don't want you to get hurt."

"I can take care of myself," Nikki replied. Hawk was about to say something else, but Nikki interrupted him. "I am going, and that is that. What time are we leaving?"

Hawk looked resigned. "We can leave around ten

tomorrow morning," he said. "I want you to wear a bulletproof vest. No argument."

"Okay," Nikki agreed. She did not think she would need a bulletproof vest, but if it made Hawk happy, she would wear one. Nikki and Hawk made dinner. Tori stopped by and told Nikki that the young man had returned.

"He loved the designer chocolates," Tori said.

"Designer chocolates?" Hawk and his father asked.

"I'll tell you about it when we eat," Nikki said. "I am glad he liked them." Seth and the chief set the table and Hawk put the food out for everyone. They all sat down, and while they ate, Nikki told them the story about the young man. Hawk and the chief laughed.

"Designer chocolates. What is this town coming to?" the chief teased.

"Oh, and I almost forgot," Nikki started. She got up from the table and grabbed her purse. She pulled out the folder and handed it to the chief. "I found this among the files."

"Thank you, Nikki," the chief replied. "I wondered where these got to."

"I was hoping you could tell me some of the stories behind those pictures," Nikki said.

"What pictures?" Seth asked. The chief pulled out one of the photos and handed it to Seth. Seth laughed.

"What are you laughing at?" Hawk asked.

"Nothing," Seth gulped. He handed the picture to Tori and she handed it to Nikki. Nikki almost spit out her tea.

"Oh, this is priceless," Nikki said.

"Let me see that," Hawk said. He grabbed the picture from Nikki. "Oh no. I thought I got rid of all these." The picture was of Hawk as a teenager with spiked hair. He had on ripped jeans and a ripped shirt.

"Was that for Halloween?" Nikki asked.

The chief guffawed. "No! That was Hawk going through his punk rock phase." Everyone laughed.

"I think it's cute," Nikki said, taking the photo back from Hawk. Hawk blushed and looked down at his dinner.

"After dinner I can go through these and tell you some more stories," the chief said.

"I would love that," Nikki replied.

"Don't we have a case to solve?" Hawk asked.

"Yes, but that can wait. Stories from your childhood trump any case, at least for tonight," Nikki replied. After dinner they cleared off the table and Seth did the dishes. Then everyone sat back down again, and the chief told them stories of Hawk and Hawk's mother. Nikki was glad for the break from the wedding and the case. Afterward, Tori went home, and everyone else went to sleep.

The next morning Nikki and Hawk drove out of town and toward a farming area to talk to suspect number one.

"I don't think I've driven out this way since I have been here," Nikki said.

"I hope you haven't," Hawk replied.

"Why not? The land looks beautiful," Nikki said.

"But the people around here are not," Hawk said. "We are going to see Jim French. My father put him in jail for dealing meth. He was released two months ago. We have been keeping an eye on him, but, so far, he has laid low. He's a nasty person, and it would not surprise me if he put a hit out on the chief. Do you have your vest on?"

"Yes, I do," Nikki said.

"Okay. I have mine on, too. This stop is why I wanted you to wear it." Hawk turned down a dirt road. After about a hundred feet the road was blocked by a massive pickup truck. Two large men with rifles stepped out. Hawk stopped his car and got out. He told Nikki to stay inside. Nikki rolled down her window so she could hear the discussion.

"State your business," the larger man said to Hawk.

"I am here to see Jim. I do not want to cause any trouble, I just want to ask him a few questions," Hawk said. The man got out his cell phone and made a call. He hung up and told Hawk to follow them. Hawk got back into his car and followed the truck down the road.

"Do you have your gun?" Hawk asked Nikki.

"Of course," Nikki answered.

"Take it out and put it into the glove compartment," Hawk said.

"Why?" Nikki answered.

"Because they will search us. I want to go in unarmed so they know we just want to ask some questions," Hawk replied. The pickup truck had stopped by a farmhouse. Hawk opened the glove compartment and put his pistol inside. Nikki put her gun next to his. They got out of the car and Hawk locked it. The two men came over and patted them down, then motioned Nikki and Hawk to follow them into the farmhouse. Nikki stayed close behind Hawk and noticed a few more armed men around the house. They went inside, and Nikki saw a man sitting at a table. He was about the chief's age.

"Hello, Hawk," the man said.

"Hello, Jim," Hawk replied.

"Are you going to introduce me to the lovely lady beside you?" Jim asked.

"Nope," said Hawk.

"Fair enough," Jim replied. "Have a seat."

"We'll stand," Hawk said. "Where were you the other day?"

"You mean the day that deputy was killed?" Jim asked. Nikki would have been surprised except she knew how quickly gossip spread in Maple Hills.

"Yes," Hawk replied.

"I was at church," Jim said. "It is out of town."

"Excuse me?" Hawk asked.

"You heard me. I have turned over a new leaf," Jim said. "I started going to church while I was in prison. I got baptized and everything. I have checked in with my parole officer each week."

"If you are so reformed, why do you have armed bodyguards?" Nikki asked.

"Good question, little lady," Jim answered. Nikki cringed when he directed his stare at her. "I have them around for my protection," Jim continued. "I stopped production and I have people who are not happy about that. I need protection from them. You know, former distributors. Former dealers and users."

"People whose lives you ruined," Hawk said.

"Now, I would not say that. I made something and they bought it. I did not force them to buy meth. They chose to buy it," Jim said. Hawk shook his head.

"I will need to know what church you went to," Hawk said. "Also, you need to make sure all of your boys have carry permits or I will be paying you another visit."

"All of these guns are legal, and they all have permits," Jim reassured Hawk. Hawk turned to go.

"Tell your father I said thank you. If he had not arrested me, I might not have turned my life around," Jim said.

Hawk shook his head again and motioned for Nikki to leave in front of him. They got back to the car and put their guns in their holsters. Hawk drove away. He called a deputy and asked him to check Jim's alibi.

"I don't believe for a minute that he turned his life around," Hawk said. "But I didn't see any equipment around that proves he is cooking again. If he quit, that will be good for the town."

"I believe people can change," Nikki said. "I don't know if he has, though."

"We'll see what the deputy finds out," Hawk said as he

drove back toward town. The next stop was the young man who had been arrested for killing his father.

"He says that his father abused him, but the chief could not find any solid evidence of abuse," Hawk told Nikki. "My father caught him red-handed with a knife over his father's body. It was enough to put him away for ten years. He got out on parole last month, and he may very well want my father dead for putting him in prison."

They drove to a small house just outside of town. Hawk and Nikki walked up to the door. They heard a dog barking in the backyard. The door opened and a man in his mid-twenties answered.

"Can I help you?" the man asked.

"I am looking for Rafael Rodriquez," Hawk said.

"That is me," the man said. Hawk introduced himself.

"Where were you three days ago? I need an account of your whereabouts for the day," Hawk said.

"Would you like to come inside?" Rafael asked.

"No, thank you. I can ask the questions out here," Hawk replied. Nikki knew that Hawk did not want to put himself or her into a dangerous situation. The man who answered the door was clean shaven and seemed a bit shy. Nikki had to remind herself that he had killed his father.

"Okay. I was working during the day and then I went to my girlfriend's house," Rafael replied after thinking about it for a few moments. "A couple of my friends were over, too. We were just hanging out watching the baseball game."

"Okay," Hawk replied. "I will need your girlfriend's and friends' names." Rafael gave them to Hawk along with their contact information. Hawk wrote the information down.

"Do not skip town," Hawk warned Rafael.

"I won't," Rafael stated. "I have a girlfriend and a good job. I check in with my parole officer. I don't want to mess anything up." Hawk and Nikki went back to the car.

"I believe him," Nikki said.

"Don't be fooled by appearances," Hawk warned.

"I have a gut feeling about this," Nikki said.

"Okay, but I still think he is a suspect," Hawk replied. He turned on the car and they drove into a nicer section of town.

"This is Tom Stuart's house," Hawk told Nikki as they drove up to a gate. Hawk pushed a button and introduced himself. The gates opened.

"This is a huge house," Nikki said. It was a mansion set in the town. Tall hedges surrounded the house and the lawn was perfectly manicured.

"How can he have this place if he was arrested for fraud?" Nikki asked Hawk.

"He does not own the house. My father could never figure out who owned it. My father thinks Tom has ties with the mob, but he was only able to arrest him on tax evasion. Tom spent his time in jail surrounded by the mafia. They took care of him and he got out on good behavior. I would not be surprised if they taught him how to take someone out while he was in there," Hawk said as they pulled up to the front door. The door opened and a man walked out. He was older than the chief, but he was in excellent shape. Hawk and Nikki got out of the car. The man met them on the front lawn.

"Hello, Hawk," Tom said.

"Hello, Tom," Hawk replied.

"What brings you around?" Tom asked.

"I need to know where you were three days ago," Hawk replied.

"I was out of town," Tom said.

"Where were you exactly?" Hawk asked.

"I was at the Clairmore Hotel," Tom said. The Clairmore hotel was a nice hotel a couple of towns away. It was located in a ski resort. It was one of those hotels Nikki knew she would never be able to afford to stay in.

"Was anyone with you? Your wife, maybe?" Hawk asked.

"No," Tom answered. "The hotel staff can vouch for my presence. I was meeting someone."

"Who were you meeting?" Hawk asked.

"That is my business," Tom replied. "You wanted me to give you my alibi, the hotel staff will tell you I was there all day."

"If I had the name of the man you were meeting with, I would be more satisfied with your alibi," Hawk answered.

"It was not a man," Tom said. "I prefer to leave the lady's name out of this discussion."

"That is fine for now," Hawk said. "Stay in town. I may need to question you again." The front door of the house opened, and an older woman stepped out.

"Tom, I didn't know we had company," the woman said to Tom.

"Martha, they were just leaving," Tom replied. The woman waved goodbye to Hawk and Nikki. Nikki and Hawk walked back to the car.

"That was suspicious," Nikki said to Hawk. "I wonder why he would not give us the woman's name he was with."

"It was probably a prostitute," Hawk said. "He might not even remember her name."

"I still think it's suspicious," Nikki said. "He was the only one to evade your questions. That puts him on the top of my list."

"I think it was either Rafael or Jim," Hawk replied. "We will check out their alibis tomorrow." Nikki agreed and asked Hawk to drop her at the chocolate shop.

"You mean your designer chocolates?" Hawk asked and laughed. Nikki hit his shoulder and laughed. She told Hawk she would meet him at her house for dinner. Hawk kissed Nikki and Nikki went into the shop. It was almost closing time, and Nikki started to help Tori and Lidia clean up the shop. Nikki noticed that most of the truffles were sold.

"They love your truffles," Lidia said. "Putting that hashtag out has gotten us some new customers."

"That's great," Nikki replied. They cleaned up and closed up the shop. Tori told Nikki that she was going to get some food to take to the house. Nikki thanked her.

"I am going to whip up some truffles and then I will be there," Nikki replied. She made the truffles and she also baked some small cakes to try the next day. Nikki knew she was cutting it close with the cake, but she wanted to solve this mystery. She put the chocolates in the refrigerator and covered the cakes to try the next day. Nikki went home and enjoyed an evening of dinner and conversation with everyone.

chapter nine

After dinner Seth asked if he could drive Tori home. He had been by the chief's side these past few days. Hawk told him to go.

"Nothing else has happened, so I think we can be without you for a couple of hours," Hawk said. Nikki agreed.

"I will be back in a little while," Seth promised. He and Tori left, and the chief offered to do the dishes.

"I'm not able to do much of anything else right now," the chief said. Nikki could tell he was getting antsy about staying at home. Hawk asked Nikki if she wanted to join him on the porch, and Nikki agreed. She brought Hawk a beer and she had a glass of wine. They sat down side by side. Nikki asked if Seth was getting Hawk's wedding arrangements set.

"Yep," Hawk replied. "He has his tux ordered and they will be delivering them to my house tomorrow. He even called the mayor and made sure the house was ready and the flowers were being delivered."

"That is wonderful," Nikki replied. She put down her wine and gave Hawk a hug and a kiss. They sat outside enjoying the fresh night air. It was a bit chilly but not cold enough for a jacket. They looked at the stars and Nikki saw a shooting star go flashing by.

"Make a wish," Hawk declared. Nikki shut her eyes and wished for the case to be done soon. Nikki and Hawk sat on the porch for a while and soon the chief joined them.

"I put away the dishes for you," the chief said.

"Thank you so much," Nikki replied. "You seem to be a bit antsy. Are you not enjoying your time off?"

The chief scowled, and Nikki and Hawk laughed.

"Don't get me wrong, I appreciate your hospitality," the chief said. "I just didn't think I would be here this long. I am starting to go a little stir crazy."

"Well, what would you say if I told you I cleared you for half a day's work tomorrow?" Hawk replied.

The chief grinned. "Since there have not been any other threats, and since we have our suspects under surveillance, I think it would be okay for you to come into the precinct for the morning," Hawk said.

The chief thanked Hawk, and Nikki could tell the chief was genuinely happy.

"I still want Seth beside you at all times," Hawk said. "Especially since we are dealing with three convicts."

"That is fine by me," the chief said. "I remember when I arrested Jim for cooking meth. His boys put up a fight, but we were able to get him without anyone getting hurt. We waited until he had left his compound. While some deputies were raiding his compound and taking his equipment, I followed him in an unmarked car. He stopped to get some groceries. I waited until he was coming out of the store and I arrested him. I had two men with me, and they took down Jim's bodyguards. It was a quick arrest, and I am glad no one was hurt. He says he stopped cooking, but I would be surprised. He made a lot of money making and distributing meth."

"He says his buyers and users are coming after him for stopping," Hawk said.

"That would make sense if he did indeed quit," the chief said. "Did you check on the permits for his guards?"

"I did," Hawk replied. "They all have permits, at least the ones who are not out on parole. Those men did not have guns when we stopped by."

"Well, maybe he is turning over a new leaf," the chief said. "Wouldn't be the strangest thing to have happened."

"I still think he could have put a hit on you," Hawk said.

"I agree," the chief replied. "Speaking of hits, how is Tom doing?"

"Martha looked well, but Tom is up to something, I am sure of it," Hawk said. "He met a woman outside of town."

"Probably a prostitute," his dad answered. Nikki grinned. *Like father, like son* she thought.

"How do we know it is not his mistress?" Nikki asked.

"Well, the last time he had a mistress his wife ran him out of town. I heard that she told him to stick to prostitutes," the chief said. Nikki asked why.

"You know what they want up front and they are less likely to talk to the police," Hawk replied.

"That actually makes a weird kind of sense," Nikki said.

"I met Rafael," Hawk said.

"He seemed nice," Nikki added.

"I truly believe that his father abused him," the chief said. "I just could never find any proof. If his father had hurt him, he did it in a way that did not leave a trace. I felt bad for Rafael and that is why I did not ask them to charge him as an adult. I still would be cautious around him."

"I agree," Hawk said. Nikki was glad to get some more background on the cases, although she wished it helped narrow down the list.

"It could be any one of them," Hawk said. The chief concurred.

Seth showed up about an hour later. The chief gave him the good news about going to work the next day. Seth was happy to be getting out of the house as well.

"I will have undercover officers around you at all times,"

Hawk promised his father and Seth. Nikki was glad to hear that. She did not want anything happening to Seth or the chief. Seth and the chief decided to go to bed. Nikki and Hawk sat out on the porch for a little while longer.

"This night is beautiful," Nikki said, snuggling next to her fiancé.

"You are beautiful," Hawk replied and tilted her head up toward his. Hawk kissed her and Nikki relaxed into his arms. They sat there for a little while longer and then Nikki said she was ready for bed. She stretched and Hawk tickled her. He kissed her again. Nikki laughed and broke free. She went inside and washed her wine glass. Hawk followed her in. He put his beer bottle in the recycle bin after rinsing it out and kissed her goodnight. Nikki went up to bed.

The next morning Nikki got up and was happy to see the chief in his uniform. Seth had made breakfast and Hawk was doing a perimeter check. They all sat down and enjoyed the bacon and eggs that Seth had made. Nikki poured everyone coffee.

"I'm sure you are happy to get back to work," Nikki said to the chief.

"I am. I enjoy a vacation, but this has felt like being in jail," the chief said. "No offense, but not being able to contact anyone and not being able to help more with the case has driven me up the wall."

"I am not surprised or offended," Nikki said. "If I had to stay somewhere and was not able to contact anyone it would drive me crazy too."

"I can't wait to get back to the station," Seth said.

"You mean you can't wait to get back near Tori," the chief said. Seth blushed and everyone laughed.

Nikki enjoyed her breakfast with the gang, and everyone got ready to leave.

"Now you know I want you back here by this afternoon," Hawk told his father. "There is still someone out there threatening you. I don't want your freedom going to your head."

"Yes, yes. I will be here," the chief replied.

"I am going to call Seth and make sure you are here," Hawk warned his father.

"We will be here. Now let me get to work," the chief said as he pushed by Hawk. Nikki laughed. Seth followed the chief and they got into Seth's car. The undercover police officers followed them into town.

"Do you need to go to the chocolate shop before we go out of town to check these leads?" Hawk asked Nikki.

"I think Lidia and Tori can handle the shop this morning," Nikki replied.

"Okay, let's roll," Hawk said. They got into Hawk's car and drove out of town.

chapter ten

Nikki and Hawk drove out of Maple Hills. The mountaintops showed a dusting of snow. Nikki was glad it had not snowed yet in Maple Hills. She knew colder weather was coming, but she hoped it would stay away until after the wedding. The leaves were turning brilliant reds and oranges and deep gold. Nikki liked looking at the different-colored leaves. It was like the mountains were wearing a crazy quilt. Nikki turned and asked Hawk where they were going first.

"We are going to stop by the church and see about Jim's alibi first. Then we will go to the hotel where Tom said he was staying," Hawk responded. They drove out to a small church in the next town. It was a stone church with a white steeple. The church was small but cute. Hawk parked the car and they went over to the side entrance. Hawk knocked on the door and it was answered by a young woman. Hawk introduced himself and Nikki. The young woman's name was Sally, and she told them she was the church's administrative assistant. She invited them into her office. Nikki followed Hawk inside, and they sat down across from Sally.

"What brings you over to our town?" Sally asked Hawk.

"I am checking on an alibi from three days ago," Hawk replied.

"Okay. We were having a benefit luncheon. I was there and I think I saw most of our guests. If it is someone I did not see, I can ask our minister," Sally replied.

"I was wondering if Jim French was at the luncheon," Hawk asked Sally.

"Not only was he at the luncheon, he was the one who put it all together. The luncheon was to benefit the youth of the church. They are going on a mission trip and Mr. French thought the church members should help them. All the proceeds from the luncheon went to funding their trip," Sally explained.

"So, Jim, I mean Mr. French, organized it? How much did you make?" Hawk asked.

"We made almost enough to fund their trip. When it was all over and the donations counted, Mr. French contributed enough money to make sure the trip was completely funded. Mr. French was here all morning getting the event organized and calling people to make sure they were going to show up," Sally replied. "He really is a generous person."

Nikki wondered if Jim was using the event to launder his drug money and she could tell that Hawk was thinking the same thing. However, this put him here and not at the crime scene. Hawk thanked Sally, and he and Nikki got back into the car.

"Maybe he has changed. I'll get a warrant to check out his finances and I'll let the chief know what Jim is up to," Hawk said.

"I was wondering if he was using the church to launder his money. That would be a new low," Nikki said. "In any case, he does have an alibi for the day Luke was killed."

"For now, I still think he could have put a hit out on my father," Hawk said. "If I can get a warrant to check his finances, we should be able to trace the money he would have paid someone to kill the chief."

"The only question I have is why the hit man killed Luke. You would think they would have had a picture of the chief," Nikki said.

"Maybe they got confused," Hawk said. "Both men have nearly the same build and both have white hair. And then when they realized they shot the wrong person, they left that threatening note about the chief."

"That makes sense," Nikki said.

They drove further from Maple Hills and decided to stop for lunch before checking their next location. Hawk knew of a little restaurant in the next town over, so they stopped there. It was a quaint town with a ski lodge and a main street. Hawk parked by the restaurant and they got out. Nikki and Hawk sat in a booth and the waitress asked what they wanted. Hawk ordered a cheeseburger and Nikki asked for a grilled chicken sandwich. They both requested coffee.

"How much do you want to bet that the chief is still in the office?" Hawk asked when the waitress left.

"I am not taking that bet," Nikki replied. One of the conditions of the chief going back to work was that he would go back to Nikki's house at lunchtime.

"We should eat our food and then you can check on him," Nikki said. Hawk laughed.

Nikki and Hawk enjoyed their lunch together. Hawk called Seth and confirmed that the chief was back at Nikki's house. Hawk and Nikki were both happy that he was back in protective custody. They left the restaurant and drove a few more hours to the hotel where Tom had stayed.

The Clairmore Hotel was a large luxury ski resort. It had valet parking, which Hawk balked at, and a grand entrance. Hawk flashed his badge and the valet driver left his car alone. Hawk and Nikki walked up to the front of the hotel. The went inside and Nikki gasped. There was a large fireplace in one corner and a bar with high-end liquor in another corner. The hotel was busy, and Hawk and Nikki made their way across the foyer.

"This reminds me of the place we stayed in for the chocolate competition," Nikki told Hawk. He agreed. They walked up to the front desk, and Nikki looked around while they were waiting to be helped. She noticed most of the clientele were middle-aged or older men. Many of them seemed to be carrying guns. Nikki was sure not to keep her eyes on anyone for too long. She turned to Hawk.

"Did you notice how many people were packing here?" Nikki asked Hawk.

"I am not surprised. This is a known mob location. We have undercover people here all the time. Usually they get caught and have to bail. Fortunately, no one has been killed on the job," Hawk replied. Nikki shivered and was glad she had her gun. A woman approached them, and Hawk asked about Tom. He showed the woman his badge and she answered his questions.

"Yes, he was here three days ago," the woman said.

"Can you tell me if he left the hotel at any time during that period?" Hawk asked. The woman typed something into her computer and shook her head.

"No," she replied. "He was here the whole time according to our valet records."

"Can you print me a copy of those records?" Hawk asked.

"I would be happy to," the woman replied.

"Was Tom here alone?" Nikki asked.

"As far as I know he was," the woman answered. Nikki's suspicions were raised.

"Are you sure he was here by himself?" she asked.

"We do not require our guests to register any names but their own. If someone was staying with Tom, or if he brought someone back to the hotel, I did not see them," the woman behind the desk informed Nikki.

"Thank you for your time and the parking registry," Hawk said. He guided Nikki away from the front desk.

"Tom admitted he was here with someone," Nikki said. "We should get a warrant to look at their security tapes."

"Maybe," Hawk answered. "I still think it was just a prostitute, though." Nikki sighed and followed Hawk to his car. They drove back toward Maple Hills. It was getting late.

"Can you drop me at my house, please?" Nikki asked Hawk. "Tori closed the shop so we should be there by dinnertime."

"Sure," Hawk replied. "I am going to go to my office and get some of these notes filed. I want to start a warrant to check into Jim's finances also."

"Okay," Nikki said. Hawk put his arm around Nikki, and she snuggled next to him for the ride back to Maple Hills.

When they arrived back at Nikki's place, Hawk dropped her off and Nikki went into her house. The chief, Seth, and Tori were there. Seth had made clam chowder and salad. Nikki dug in and filled the chief in on what they had found out. The chief was happy that Hawk was getting a warrant to look into Jim's finances.

"I had hoped he had changed his ways," the chief said. "We will see soon enough."

"I hate to say it, but with all this running around, we might have to consider postponing the wedding. We are no closer to finding out who killed Luke," Nikki said.

"I actually agree. I am afraid this is getting to be too much for you," the chief said. "If you need to postpone the wedding, I will support you." Nikki was happy to have his support. She decided to see how the next day went before making a decision.

They ate dinner and Tori filled Nikki in on the day's business. They had a few new customers at the chocolate shop. Tori's designer chocolate marketing campaign was working. Nikki just hoped she could live up to the reputation.

Nikki was glad she had Tori and Lidia to handle the shop while she was helping Hawk. Tori and Seth seemed closer than ever, and Nikki was happy about that. After dinner Nikki told everyone she was going back to the shop to work on the cake. The wedding day was fast approaching, and if Nikki did not postpone the wedding, she wanted to make sure the cake was good to go. Nikki and Seth cleared the table while the chief and Tori took care of the dishes.

"You have been running around all day," Seth told Nikki as he grabbed some plates. "Are you sure you want to go back into town? It is getting dark, and I don't want you stressing out."

"Getting some work done on the cake will actually help me relieve some of this stress," Nikki told Seth. Seth told Nikki he understood. They took the plates and bowls into the kitchen. Nikki helped dry the dishes and put them away. Once everything was set, Nikki announced she was leaving.

Tori said she would stay with Seth and the chief until Nikki got back. Nikki thanked her and she let them know that Hawk should be there soon. Nikki put her jacket on, grabbed her purse, and went outside. She waved to the police officers keeping watch and they waved back. Nikki was glad there was a police presence besides Seth at the house. Everything had been quiet, but Nikki would not rest until Luke's killer was caught. She was proud of how much Seth had grown since moving to Maple Hills. He was enjoying his job, and Nikki knew he was a good police officer. Nikki unlocked her car. She tossed her cell phone and purse onto the driver's seat and sat down. Nikki turned on the car and drove toward town.

The road to town was winding and had a few sharp turns and drop-offs on the shoulder. Nikki was always cautious when driving to town. She did not want to hit a deer or be hit by anything. The night was cloudless, and Nikki had a good view of the road ahead. Nikki noticed a car behind her. Nikki tensed up but realized It was following along at a reasonable distance. Nikki relaxed and turned on the radio. She drove another mile.

Suddenly the inside of Nikki's car grew brighter as the car behind her sped up. Nikki was coming to a turn, so she slowed down. *If you want to pass that badly go ahead, but do it before the turn,* Nikki thought. All of a sudden Nikki heard the other car's engine revving. Nikki felt a large bump that made her let go of the steering wheel. She felt her car moving toward the side of the road. On the other side of the shoulder was a ravine. Nikki grabbed the steering wheel and tried to steer away from the shoulder, but she felt another bump. Her stomach lurched as her car flew off the side of the road. Nikki screamed as the car flew through the air. The car landed in the ravine and she was knocked unconscious.

chapter eleven

When Nikki came to, everything seemed wrong. The inside of the car was dark, and Nikki's head hurt. It took a few minutes for her to realize she was upside down. The car had landed on its roof. Nikki's airbag had deployed and was in her face and pinning her arms to her sides. Her seatbelt was still on and she was hanging down. Her hair was in her face and her head was pushing against the top of the car. The roof of the car was on the ground, and Nikki was hanging above it. Nikki started to panic. Before she went crazy, she closed her eyes and thought for a moment. She took a few deep breaths. She was dizzy, and her ankle was throbbing. She was scared that she had broken it. Nikki tried to take her seatbelt off, but it did not budge. Before Nikki could begin to panic for real, she took some deep, slow breaths and calmed down.

Nikki felt hot and she grew concerned that there was a fire nearby. Then she remembered she had a knife in her pocket. Nikki had to wedge her hand around the airbag to get it into her front pocket. After a few seconds Nikki felt the edge of her pocket. She tried to jam her fingers in it but, since she was upside down, it took a bit of wiggling. She got her fingers into her pocket and felt her knife. She carefully pulled it out of her pocket. Nikki knew if the knife slipped out of her fingers she would be stuck where she was until someone found her. Nikki got her fingers around the pocketknife and gently tugged it free from her jeans. It did not drop, and Nikki breathed a sigh of relief. She maneuvered her hand close to her face and pulled the pocketknife open with her teeth. She punctured the air bag and it deflated, leaving Nikki with a view out of her shattered windshield. Nikki was happy to see that her headlights were on. She felt in her pocket for her cell phone, but it wasn't there. She tried to disengage the seatbelt again, but it was wedged into the door.

After what seemed like an hour, Nikki was able to cut herself out of her seatbelt. Her body fell down and Nikki screamed in pain. She tried to open the door, but it would not budge. She felt warmer and she started to panic. She took a deep breath and looked up. Both airbags had deployed. Nikki punctured the other bag and, when it had deflated, she opened her glove compartment. Nikki kept a window-shattering tool in her glove compartment, and it fell next to her on the roof. Nikki grabbed it and used it to puncture the driver's side window. The window shattered, and Nikki carefully shimmied out of the broken window. The impact of the collision had pushed the roof of the car down and there was not much room. Nikki moved back to the window and cleared the remaining glass out of the pane after she had gotten out and looked back inside the car. She saw her purse and her cell phone. She reached in and grabbed them and crawled backward away from the car.

Nikki sat down and looked at her ankle. She did not see any cuts or bone, so she knew she did not have a compound fracture. Nikki realized she could see her ankle even in the dark. Nikki looked toward the car and realized there was indeed a fire, and it was spreading. She tried to use her cell phone but there was no signal. She turned on the flashlight function on her phone and looked at the car. Nikki knew she had to stand up and get moving. She looked around and saw a large stick lying nearby. She crawled over and used the stick to stand up. When she stood up, she saw flames near the back of her car.

As Nikki was standing up, she smelled something. Nikki sniffed again and grew pale. She smelled gasoline. Nikki hobbled as fast as she could away from the car. She thought about the wedding and the cake. Nikki realized that the cake was not important. Being with Hawk was the most important thing. She almost tripped over some stones, but she maintained her balance and kept going. She could still smell the gasoline and she could feel her back getting warmer. Nikki tried to hobble faster. She threw her purse and hobbled after it. Nikki heard a loud bang and felt a rush of hot air hit her on the back. Nikki's head jerked back as her body was pushed forward. Nikki fell and was knocked unconscious again.

chapter twelve

Nikki was dreaming. She and Hawk were having a campfire by the lake. Nikki watched as Hawk put another log on the fire. Nikki stood up and was reaching for Hawk when she felt herself falling backward into the fire. She woke up screaming.

Nikki opened her eyes and tasted dirt. She spat out the dirt and tried to move her head. Her head was throbbing, and it took her a minute to remember what happened. Nikki felt stones beneath her head and neck. She remembered the wreck and got angry. She tried to remember exactly what had happened, but everything was a jumble in her head. She remembered getting out of the car and the explosion. Her back felt sore and she wondered how badly it was burned. Nikki looked toward the car. It was engulfed in flames. The blast had blown her away from the fire. Nikki had to get help. *Surely someone heard the crash or saw the flames,* Nikki thought. She tried to stand up but fainted from the pain.

Nikki opened her eyes once again. Her head was banging and her whole body hurt. She looked over toward her car. The fire had lessened somewhat. Nikki sat and listened. She heard frogs and crickets above the fire but no other sounds. A minute later Nikki thought she heard a siren, but it turned out to be an owl swooping down near the fire. Nikki felt around and found her phone. She turned it on but there was no service. Nikki had hoped that someone would have noticed the fire and called 911. Since the fire was lower, Nikki knew she had been out for a while. If help had been coming it would have been here by now. Nikki felt around her head. She pulled her hand back and looked at it. There was blood all over her hand. Nikki needed to get help fast.

Nikki had lost her stick in the fall. She used her phone to locate it. She strapped her purse on her back and slowly inched toward the stick over the rocky terrain. Nikki felt the skin on her knees tear, and she tried not to scream. She didn't want to waste her energy screaming. Nikki got close to the stick and she reached out and grabbed ahold of it. It was a minor victory, but she felt like an Olympic gold medalist. Her head flared and she rested. She felt drowsy but she jerked her head up. Nikki knew she could not afford to fall asleep. She stuck the stick firmly on the ground and tried to use it to get into a kneeling position, but her ankle flared up and her knees were sore from the rocks. Nikki yelped and sat back down.

She knew she had to get help soon. She took off her jacket and wrapped it tightly around her ankle. This provided a brace to keep her ankle in place. She knew she would have to grit through the pain in her knees. Slowly, Nikki was able to kneel with the help of the stick. She let herself yelp a couple of times and then took a deep breath. She tried her phone again but there was still no signal. *Maybe if I stand up, it will work,* Nikki thought. With that in mind, Nikki planted her foot in front of her and used the stick to maneuver into a standing position. That was when she really felt her back pain. Nikki was not sure if the pain was from burns or if she had wrenched her back.

Nikki tried her phone again and it still did not work. Nikki realized she would need to get out of the ravine in order to get a signal. Nikki looked up. Her head and ankle throbbed. Nikki knew that right at this moment, she could sit down and go to sleep and possibly never wake up, or she could climb. Nikki chose to climb. She chose to climb for herself, for Seth, and for Hawk. Nikki would never give up. Hawk said her tenaciousness was one of her most endearing qualities. It was in that moment that Nikki knew she wanted to marry Hawk more than anything else in the whole world. She would climb up the ravine and make it down the aisle as scheduled.

Nikki was determined to get up the ravine. She put her phone in her pocket and made sure her purse was attached. She put the stick forward and inched up to the side of the ravine. If the ravine had been clear cut, Nikki would not have stood a chance; however, it was rugged, and it rose to the road. There were footholds in the ravine and scrub bushes that Nikki could use to help in her ascent. Nikki slowly inched her way forward using her hands and the stick to keep on track. She pulled herself up carefully, losing her footing a couple of times. The last time, her stick fell back down into the ravine. Nikki was cold and it was hard to keep a grip on the bushes. She almost gave up and followed the stick back down but then she remembered Hawk and Seth. She needed to get help. Nikki would get back to Hawk and Seth if it was the last thing she did.

"I am not dying here," Nikki shouted.

Her yell scared a nearby racoon and she glimpsed its mask as it ran down the ravine. Nikki ground her teeth. She took all the anger and stress she was feeling and channeled them into climbing up the last five feet.

When she reached the top of the ravine, Nikki pulled herself over and onto the shoulder of the road. She could not kneel or stand. She lay there as a wave of dizziness overcame her. Nikki noticed some lights and thought she was getting a migraine. She realized it was an approaching car. A car was coming, and Nikki's spirits lifted. She could not stand without the stick, but she waved her hands wildly as she lay on the asphalt. The car passed by, not even slowing down. Nikki did not give up. She reached into her jeans pocket and was relieved to feel her cell phone. She pulled out her phone and her heart gave a leap. There was a signal! Her head was pounding, and her ankle was screaming, but Nikki was able to find Hawk's number and dial. The phone rang and Nikki was worried that it was going to go to voicemail. She felt another dizzy spell coming on. As the dizziness struck, she heard a voice.

"Nikki, where are you?" Hawk asked. Nikki heard Hawk and tried to answer. She started to cry and then she passed out.

chapter thirteen

Nikki opened her eyes. She heard a beeping noise and saw a bright light. Nikki thought she was still on the side of the road, but the light was too bright. Maybe she was about to be hit by a car. Nikki panicked. She lurched and felt a hand on her shoulder.

"Easy does it," Hawk said. Nikki realized she was in the hospital. The room came into focus and she saw Hawk standing above her. She saw that she had an IV in her arm and some machines were beeping by her bed. Nikki started to cry. Hawk held her in his arms. She sobbed for a bit and then dried her tears. She was feeling completely exhausted and sore all over. Nikki looked around. The chief and Seth were in the room as well.

"You're going to be okay," she heard Hawk say.

"What happened?" Nikki asked. The chief and Seth visibly relaxed when Nikki spoke.

"What do you remember?" Hawk asked.

"I remember there was a car accident. I had to climb up the side of the ravine. I heard your voice and I passed out."

"Is that all you can remember?" Hawk asked.

Nikki thought for a moment. "No!" she exclaimed. "Someone pushed my car off of the road. I was driving into town to go to the chocolate shop and someone hit my car. They hit it again and sent it over the edge. I woke up and I was upside down. I cut myself out of the seatbelt and deflated the airbags with my knife. I broke the driver's side window and got out of the car. I found my cell phone but there was no signal. I tried to get up, but my ankle was sore." She stopped. "Is my ankle broken?" she asked.

"No," Hawk said. "The doctor took an X-ray after they put some fluids into you. You were very dehydrated." Nikki breathed a sigh of relief and then she continued talking.

"I got out of the car and managed to get a large stick. I used that to help me stand up and keep my balance. When I was up, I moved a little and I smelled gas. I started to get away from the car and it exploded." Seth winced, and Nikki stopped, feeling tears in her eyes. She continued.

"I woke up and thought someone must have heard the crash. If they were driving by, they might see the flames. I thought help was on the way. I tried to get up, but I could not really move. I passed out again. When I woke up, I realized no one was coming. I had to find my purse and my stick. I knew I had to get up to the top of the ravine or I would be in trouble. I thought of you and Seth and got up. I moved slowly but was able to get to the side of the ravine. The bottom of the ravine was full of rocks and I stumbled a few times. I got to the side of the ravine and I climbed up even though it hurt, and I felt like passing out. The thought of you and Seth got me through the climb. I got to the top and fell over from pain and exhaustion. A car drove past. I tried to wave it down, but it kept on going. I pulled out my cell phone and passed out. That is all I remember," Nikki said.

"That is a lot to remember," Hawk said. "Let me fill you in on what happened after you pulled your cell phone out. You called me and I knew you were in trouble. You were crying and then I did not hear anything. I kept yelling your name, but you did not respond. I knew you were in trouble. When I got to your house and you were not there, I tried calling your cell phone. It went right to voicemail. I tried calling you at the chocolate shop when I could not reach you on your cell. There was no answer at the shop, and I was starting to get worried. When you called, the chief got ahold of someone at the precinct. We used your phone's GPS to track your location. Meanwhile, a helicopter was dispensed to your house to take me to the location. When the location pinged, I was already in the helicopter and we took off. A couple of minutes later we landed in the road near you. When I hopped out of the plane, I saw you on the side of the road and I ran to you. You were passed out. An ambulance had been deployed to the location and it arrived a few minutes later. The paramedics got to work on you, and they took you to the hospital. Meanwhile, the chopper went down into the ravine to find your car. I am sorry to say that your car is totaled, but I guess you knew that."

"I kind of figured I would not be driving it again." Nikki grinned slightly. Hawk rolled his eyes and the chief and Seth laughed.

"What is my prognosis?" Nikki asked.

"The doctor said you have some second-degree burns on your back, but they will heal quickly. Your ankle is sprained, not broken, and you have a mild concussion," the chief said. "Also, you have abrasions on your knees and hands, but the rest of you is fine." Nikki was relieved that her injuries were not as extensive as she had thought.

Nikki asked about the IV.

"It's because you were a bit dehydrated when they brought you in," Seth replied.

At that moment a nurse walked in and told Nikki she would be removing the IV. Nikki thanked her and was grateful to have the needle out of her arm.

"I told them you did not want any major pain

medications," Seth said. Nikki thanked him. She wanted her head to be clear.

"You need to stay in the hospital for a day or two so they can observe you," the chief said.

"A day or two?" Nikki exclaimed. "I have to get things ready for the wedding. I survived this wreck. I am not postponing my wedding."

"Lidia and Tori are working on things for you," Seth said. "You have to stay here and rest. The doctor does not want anything else happening to you. No arguments."

Nikki realized she was lucky to be alive, so she did not complain.

"Top of my list is finding out who did this. I am going to check around local garages and see if anyone brought their car in for repairs today. Specifically, front end damage," Hawk said. "I will be back soon. Listen to the doctors." Hawk gave Nikki a kiss and left. After he left, Nikki motioned the chief and Seth closer to the bed.

"Does he know why I went back to the chocolate shop?" Nikki asked Seth.

"No. We didn't tell him you were going to work on the cake. He assumed you went back to make more chocolates for the store," Seth replied.

"Thank you," Nikki said, relieved. She knew it was petty to worry about, but she wanted to have one surprise for Hawk.

"Oh no." Nikki realized something. "If I am stuck in the hospital, I won't be able to finish Hawk's cake in time." Nikki started to panic and then she saw Lidia. Lidia had arrived in time to hear Nikki's lament.

Lidia went over to Nikki's bed. She gave Nikki a gentle hug.

"Don't worry about the cake. I am taking care of it," Lidia told Nikki.

"But how?" Nikki asked.

"Just consider it my gift to you. You need to rest and heal. We have all the wedding plans under control," Lidia promised. Nikki started to cry. Lidia held her.

"You are such a dear friend. What would I do without you?" Nikki asked Lidia.

Soon, the chief and Seth said they were going back to Nikki's.

"We will get you a change of clothes and some better food," the chief said. Nikki thanked them. They left and Lidia sat on the bed by Nikki.

Lidia spent some time consoling Nikki. She reassured her that the plans for the wedding were moving along smoothly. Nikki was worried about the cake. She had some specific ideas in mind. Nikki thought about it and figured it did not matter what the cake looked like. Nikki was just glad to be around to have some. Nikki was also glad that Lidia was around to help her in her time of need. Nikki dried her eyes and asked Lidia about the chocolate shop. Lidia was filling her in on the day's sales when suddenly Nikki remembered something.

"Where is my phone?" Nikki asked Lidia. Lidia looked around and found Nikki's phone. Lidia handed it to her. Nikki called Hawk.

"Is everything okay?" Hawk asked.

"Yes. I was just wondering about Rafael's alibi," Nikki said. Hawk was going to stop by Rafael's house after work.

"His alibi checks out. He was hanging with his girlfriend all day and all night long," Hawk replied. "There were several noise complaints throughout the night, and he was there each time the police were called. They were just playing their music loud. Other people stopped by and the neighbor who lives beside Rafael's girlfriend confirmed that Rafael was there all day. The neighbor saw Rafael come out of the apartment the next morning."

"Okay. Thank you," Nikki said. She was glad that Rafael

was cleared, but she was anxious because they still had no new leads in Luke's killer or the chief's threat or the person who ran Nikki off the road. Nikki felt if they were not the same person, then they were working together. Nikki felt a bit dizzy. She knew she probably should not sleep, but she needed some rest.

"I am feeling a bit tired," Nikki told Lidia.

"Why don't you get some rest. I am going back to the chocolate shop," Lidia replied. "I don't want to leave Tori by herself for too long. We are getting more and more new customers by the day."

"That is excellent," said Nikki, yawning. Lidia said goodbye and Nikki drifted off, trying to remember anything about the car that hit her. Nikki slept. While she was sleeping, she dreamed of a woman with red hair screaming at her. Nikki woke up with a start and called Hawk.

chapter fourteen

Nikki waited in the hospital for Hawk. She had called him with some information and Hawk dropped everything. Hawk told Nikki he would be there soon. Nikki kept thinking about the accident and was hoping that some more information would present itself to her. She thought about the wreck and she tried to piece together the moments before the car went off the shoulder. Hawk appeared.

"So, what do you remember?" Hawk asked Nikki.

"It was a dream, but it was so real," Nikki said. "I saw a woman with red hair in a car beside me screaming at me. Could I really have seen that?"

"I suppose the driver could have been visible right before you left the road, and it's only now coming through your subconscious mind. At this point I will take any leads I can get," Hawk replied. He sat on the bed and gently moved some of Nikki's hair off of her face. Nikki was so happy by the gentle touch that she felt her eyes water up again. Hawk wiped Nikki's eyes and kissed them. She settled down and kissed Hawk.

"Did you find out about any cars needing repairs?" Nikki asked Hawk.

"I went to John's Motors and they had a car that had been in an accident, but the damage was in the rear. The front bumper was pristine. I drove over to Chuck's place and he did not have any new repairs." Hawk had driven to two other mechanics and their stories were the same. Hawk asked them to call him if anyone appeared with a damaged front end. All of the mechanics promised to do so.

"I am going back to the office to see if a redheaded woman was mentioned in any of the files from my father's former cases that we pulled."

"I really want to get out of here and help you," Nikki said. "I am tired of being in this bed."

"I know, but you can't leave without a doctor's permission," Hawk said.

Nikki felt like she was hitting brick walls. "Now I know how the chief feels. Can't you talk to the doctor and convince him I am ready to leave?" Nikki asked. "Let him know that I will stay off my feet, but I want to be in my own home."

"I think he knows you well enough to know you will try and get back to work," Hawk said and chuckled.

"I won't, I promise, at least for the rest of the day and tomorrow morning. I just want to be somewhere where I can rest and not be poked and prodded every thirty minutes. I know the nurses and doctors are only doing their job, but I want to go home," Nikki insisted. Hawk looked at her. Nikki knew Hawk realized how stubborn she could be. Hawk sighed.

"I know that look in your eyes. Before you try and break yourself out of this hospital, let me talk to the doctor. If he clears you, I will drive you home," Hawk told Nikki.

Nikki smiled. "Thank you," she said. She felt better knowing she might get out of the hospital soon.

"I believe the doctor is doing his rounds on the other floors. Let me check the files and I promise I will talk to the doctor as soon as I am done," Hawk said. Nikki reluctantly agreed. She knew if she pushed the doctor too hard, he would keep her in the hospital longer. Nikki resigned herself to her afternoon hospital stay.

Hawk gave Nikki a hug and kiss and left her alone in her hospital room. Nikki tried to rest in her bed, and she drifted into a light sleep. She woke up suddenly. The door was opening. Nikki hoped Hawk was back, but instead a nurse walked in.

Seeing Nikki's dejected look, the nurse asked, "Were you expecting someone else?"

"I'm sorry," Nikki replied. "I thought you might be my ride out of here." The nurse smiled and checked Nikki's chart.

"Would you like me to get you a snack while you are waiting for your ride?" the nurse asked Nikki. "I have noticed your impressive visitors. It's not everyone who has the chief of police and a handsome detective visiting them." Nikki smiled and thanked the nurse.

"I think I have some change in my purse." Nikki started looking around for it.

"That's okay. I have some change. Would you like some chocolate?" the nurse asked. "I am sure they are not as good as yours, but it is chocolate."

"You know me?" Nikki asked.

"I know your shop, and I put two and two together when I saw your name," the nurse answered.

"Thank you. Some chocolate would be great," Nikki replied with a smile. The nurse left, and Nikki realized how lucky she was to have the chief and Hawk in her life, not to mention Lidia and Tori. Nikki had some of the best friends on the planet. She was feeling happy and smiling when the door opened again. It was the chief.

"What are you smiling about? I am not complaining, I love to see you smile," the chief said. "I brought you a change of clothes and some snacks from home."

"I was just thinking how lucky I am to have you and

Hawk in my life," Nikki said. "You have taken Seth and me in and made us a part of your family. I don't know if I really thanked you for that. Thank you, Chief."

The chief had a duffel bag in his hand. He put the bag down by the bed and gave Nikki a gentle hug. "Thank you for being such a great person. I have never seen my son so happy before," he said.

"He makes me happy, too," Nikki replied. She saw the nurse come in. Nikki frowned when she noticed that the nurse locked the door. Before Nikki could say anything, the nurse pulled out a gun and walked over to Nikki's bedside. The nurse aimed the gun at the chief. Thinking quickly, Nikki swung her leg out of the bed and hit the nurse. Nikki kicked the nurse in her abdomen and the nurse bent over and dropped the gun. The chief dove for the gun but the nurse dove, too. They both reached it at the same time. The chief and the nurse struggled for possession of the gun. Nikki heard some yelling and banging. She tried to get out of the bed to help the chief, but she was caught up in her blankets. Both the chief and the nurse had their hands on the gun, each trying to wrestle it out of the other person's hand. The chief tried to push the nurse, but he could not get any traction on the slippery floor. Just as the chief started to lose his grip, the door burst open. Seth and Hawk came running into the room. Seth jumped on the nurse's back and Hawk grabbed the gun from her. Seth cuffed the nurse and Hawk helped the chief up off of the floor. The chief fell into a nearby chair, panting, while Seth cuffed the nurse. Nikki untangled herself from the sheets and looked at the nurse. There were some red hairs around her face.

"Hawk, she has red hair," Nikki told Hawk. "I think she is wearing a wig." Hawk turned and pulled on the nurse's hair. She was indeed wearing a wig, and it flew off.

"You must be Penny Hatcher," Hawk said to the nurse. The nurse scowled.

"Who is Penny Hatcher?" Nikki asked.

"Penny Hatcher was seeing Rafael's father on the side. I saw her mentioned in Rafael's file. I called Rafael and he said he had never heard of her," Hawk said.

"Yeah, I am Penny," the woman said. "I know that Rafael shot his father. All his father did was slap him around a little. The jury should have given Rafael the death sentence. Instead, they let him go into juvenile detention. My sweetheart was dead because of that boy and all he got was a slap on the wrist. I wanted to kill Rafael to avenge his father, but I could not get near him. He was always with his girlfriend or his friends. He was never alone long enough for me to get near him."

"What do you mean Rafael's father slapped him around?" The chief interrupted Penny's rant.

"His father was just trying to slap some sense into him. Rafael accused him of being a drunk. Rafael's father socked him in the stomach. He liked doing that because it did not leave any marks on the kid. I thought the kid was learning but then he had to go and shoot his father. I never met Rafael, but his father would tell me what he had to do to keep Rafael in line," Penny said.

Nikki was horrified. The chief had turned pale.

"He was abused," Nikki heard the chief murmur.

"What did you do when you could not get to Rafael?" Hawk asked Penny.

"I went after the chief. After all, it is his fault that Rafael was not still in jail. He did all he could to persuade the judge and jury that Rafael was not a bad person. I scoped out the police department and learned the chief's schedule. I put on a wig and walked into the police station. I pretended to sell calendars for charity. While I was talking to the receptionist, I heard the chief making plans with the officer. I heard him giving directions to the cabin and knew I would finally have my revenge. I went to the cabin early and waited. A car came by and someone got out. The person looked like the chief, so I shot him. When I realized my mistake, I wrote a note to the chief. I wanted him to know I was gunning for him and then I left. The next day I walked by the precinct and heard that the chief was not at his house. I didn't know where he was, but I noticed that you two were getting cozy." Here, Penny pointed to Hawk and Nikki. "I followed you home and noticed the officers keeping watch outside. I knew the chief was there, but I could not get to him. I tried on the day he went to town but there were too many cops. I decided to go after Nikki to lure the chief out again. I followed her down the road and rammed her. I waited and circled back a few times. I thought you might be dead. I was glad to see you on the side of the road."

"You were the car that drove by me and ignored me," Nikki said.

"Yep. I thought the chief would appear. Instead it was only him." Penny pointed to Hawk. "He came to your rescue. I thought for sure I would never have a chance to get the chief and then I had an idea. I knew if I got into this room, I could kill the chief."

"But Nikki kicked her and sent the gun flying," the chief said.

"And then Hawk and Seth broke the door down," Nikki added. "I wondered what that noise was. Thank you for saving us." Hawk hugged Nikki as Seth dragged Penny up off the floor.

"I am taking her to jail," Seth said.

"I am going with you," the chief added. They marched Penny out of Nikki's room.

Nikki was thrilled. They had solved the case and no one else had been injured. Nikki winced as she lay back down. Hawk looked at her foot.

"Is this the leg you used to kick Penny?" Hawk asked.

"Yes," Nikki replied.

"You might need another X-ray," Hawk said.

"Why?" Nikki asked. She then realized she had kicked Penny with her sprained ankle.

"I'm okay," Nikki reassured Hawk. "I didn't hear anything snap." Hawk rolled his eyes.

"At least you can now stay here for another night," Hawk said.

"No way," Nikki said. "I still want to go home. The case is solved, and the wedding will go on as planned. And I was able to help you catch the killer. If I could do that, surely I don't belong in a hospital bed!"

Hawk sighed. "There is nothing I can say to change your mind, is there?"

"Not a thing," Nikki said. "Now, are you going to find a doctor or am I going to break out of here?"

"Fine," Hawk said. "Stay here and I will go and get a doctor."

Hawk left and Nikki got out of bed. She hopped over to the bag the chief had brought her. Nikki opened it and took out a change of clothes. She hobbled to the bathroom and got changed. By the time Hawk got back with the doctor, Nikki had her boots on and was ready to go. The doctor made her take off her boots and he examined her ankle.

"It is not broken," the doctor said. "I would like you to stay here so I can monitor you, but I know how stubborn you can be. So I am going to discharge you. You have to use crutches for the next couple of days." Nikki thanked him and put on her boots. A nurse came in with some crutches. Nikki hobbled out and Hawk grabbed her bag. He followed her down the hallway and outside.

"I will bring the car around. Stay here," Hawk ordered.

"Yes, sir." Nikki beamed. She was excited. Her wedding was a couple of days away and she would be there. So would the chief. Everything was coming together.

chapter fifteen

Nikki woke up. The sun was shining brightly, and she stretched before bouncing out of bed. Today was the day. Seth had slept over at Hawk's house, and Lidia and Tori had spent the night at Nikki's. Nikki was excited. She was also a bit nervous. She went downstairs using the railing and a crutch to support her ankle and smelled coffee brewing. Tori and Lidia had whipped up a breakfast fit for a queen. Lidia had made crepes and Tori had cut up fresh fruit and made a sauce to go with the crepes. Nikki was stunned.

"Only the best for the best," Lidia said as Nikki walked into the kitchen. Nikki had not been sure she would be able to eat breakfast, but she could not resist the delicacies in front of her. Nikki sat down and ate with Lidia and Tori. After breakfast, Nikki went upstairs to get ready. She took a shower and styled her hair. Tori helped Nikki with her makeup since Nikki's hands were shaking. Afterward, Nikki sat on her bed thinking.

"I'm here to help you get dressed," Lidia said, coming into the room. "What are you doing sitting still? You have to get ready."

"I am trying to think of something borrowed and blue," Nikki replied. "Like the rhyme."

"Okay. Something old, something new, something borrowed, something blue. What do you have and what do you still need?"

"Well," Nikki replied, "something old is my engagement ring. Something new is my dress."

"Here is something borrowed," Lidia said. "Turn around." Nikki did what she was told and felt Lidia tug her hair.

"Now look in the mirror," Lidia commanded. Nikki did. Her hair had been swept up and secured by a beautiful hair pin. It was diamond studded and sparkled in the sunlight.

"It's beautiful," Nikki breathed.

"I wore it at my wedding. I hope you have the same happiness that I have had," Lidia replied. Nikki hugged her.

"Okay, now I just need something blue," Nikki said.

"Here you go," said Tori, coming into the bedroom. She handed Nikki a box. Nikki opened it and blushed a little. Inside the box was a lace garter with a light blue ribbon intertwined within the lace.

"It is beautiful and perfect," Nikki said to Tori. They all giggled.

"We will be downstairs. Let us know if you need anything," Lidia said to Nikki. Nikki thanked them and turned to her dress. Nikki had chosen a beautiful rose-colored silk dress that was off the shoulders with long sleeves. Nikki knew the weather would be cold, and since the wedding was being held outside, she chose a long sleeve dress so she would not end up wearing a coat. Nikki put on the garter and slid the dress on. She called for Lidia. Lidia came upstairs and helped her zip up the dress. Nikki walked downstairs using her crutches, and Tori gasped.

"You look beautiful," Tori exclaimed. Nikki thanked her. She was glad she had gotten flats for the wedding. Heels would have been a no go. Lidia checked the time.

"Are you ready?" Lidia asked Nikki.

"I am," Nikki replied. Lidia drove Nikki to the park and Tori followed in her car. When they arrived, Nikki got out of the car.

"You need your crutches," Lidia scolded, noticing Nikki had left them in the car.

"I am not walking down the aisle with crutches," Nikki insisted.

"Fine, but at least use them to get to the gazebo," Lidia said. Nikki sighed but got her crutches from the car. She limped over to the gazebo. The gazebo was decorated perfectly. There were fall-colored lights around the edges of the roof and the chairs were all draped in ivory fabric. Someone had strewn rose petals down the aisle and Nikki loved the effect. The chief was there waiting for her at the back end of the aisle. He had on his dress blues.

Nikki whistled. "Don't you look dapper."

"And you are pretty as a picture," the chief replied. Nikki thanked him. Tori slipped by and went to find her seat. A local violinist started to play, and Lidia walked down the aisle.

"I am leaving my crutches here," Nikki told the chief. "Can you support me?"

"I will carry you down this aisle if I have to," the chief replied. Nikki snickered. She ditched her crutches and took the chief's arm. They paused at the back of the aisle, and Nikki looked up. There were a number of people on both sides of the aisle and the chairs were full. Nikki looked to the front of the gazebo and caught her breath. Hawk was dressed to nines in his tuxedo with tails. He looked so handsome.

"Are you ready?" the chief asked.

"You bet," Nikki said. She walked slowly down the aisle with the chief. When they reached Hawk, the chief took her hand and passed it to Hawk. Hawk leaned down and whispered into Nikki's ear.

"You look ravishing," he said. Nikki blushed deeply, filled with excitement. She couldn't believe the day had finally arrived. The mayor presided over the service, and Nikki and Hawk read simple vows. Everyone clapped and cheered when Nikki and Hawk kissed at the end. Nikki and Hawk walked down the aisle into a limousine provided by the mayor. There were champagne and two glasses in the back. Hawk poured Nikki a glass and poured one for himself. The limousine driver drove around the town for a little while to allow the guests to get to the mayor's house for the reception. Nikki liked the peace and quiet of the ride.

"To us," Hawk said as he raised his glass. Nikki raised hers, and the glasses met with a clink. Nikki sipped some of the champagne. She and Hawk kissed, and Nikki leaned against him.

"Did you think we would pull this off with everything else happening?" Nikki asked.

"I never doubted it," Hawk replied.

Nikki kissed him. "That's why I love you."

The driver pulled into the mayor's driveway. Nikki had no idea what she was walking into. Hawk helped Nikki out of the car, and they walked into the mayor's house. Practically everyone from the town was inside. Nikki and Hawk walked into a standing ovation. Cries of "Speech" were heard, but Nikki just wanted to sit down with Hawk. She was feeling overwhelmed but in a good way. Hawk guided her to a table with Lidia, Seth, Tori, and the chief.

"Let me get you something to eat," Hawk said.

"Thank you," Nikki replied. The champagne had made her a bit dizzy. Nikki saw the buffet table. It was full of wonderful fall food. Lidia had arranged all of the food and decorations. Tori and Seth helped prepare the food. Nikki saw fried clams, sautéed clams, steaks, and ham. There were sides of collards and squash. Tori had carved out pumpkins and they were being used to hold the salad dressing and other condiments. There were real fall leaves all over the table. Nikki loved the buffet. She looked around the room. The mayor's wife had decorated the mansion in a fall decor. There were leaves all around, wreaths, and gourds. Candles were on every conceivable surface and provided soft lighting for the dinner. Nikki thought about the cake but put it out of her mind. It didn't matter what the cake looked like. Being married to Hawk was the most important thing of all.

Hawk reappeared with a plate and a glass of juice for Nikki. Nikki enjoyed the food and talked to everyone who stopped by the table. After they ate, Nikki and Hawk went around the house saying hello to everyone. In one room Nikki saw a table piled high with presents.

"Are all of those for us?" Nikki asked Hawk.

"Yes, they are," Hawk said. "We are one popular couple." Nikki laughed. She could not believe all the people who had come out for the wedding and the reception.

"Hawk, Nikki," Nikki heard Lidia cry. She pulled Hawk back toward the table.

"Come and sit down, it is time for the cake," Lidia said. Nikki felt a stab of melancholy but brushed it off. She had really wanted to surprise Hawk. The cake was going to mean so much to him. Nikki and Hawk sat at the table. A door opened and Nikki saw the front of a cart being pushed out. Lidia was guiding the cart and Seth and Tori were on either side blocking the cake. Nikki moved back and forth but she could not see the cake or who was pushing the cart. All of a sudden Lidia, Tori, and Seth dropped away. Nikki and everyone else gasped. Sylvia from the chocolate competition was standing there. In front of her was the exact cake that Nikki was going to make.

"Wait. How did you do this? Sylvia?" Nikki stuttered. Sylvia came over and gave Nikki a hug.

"Your dear friend Lidia called and told me your cake predicament. I came over a few days ago and took a look at your sketches and notes. I pieced this together. I hope it is everything you wanted," Sylvia said to Nikki. "You helped me at the chocolate competition, and I felt I owed you a favor. It was my honor to make this for your special day."

Nikki was speechless. So was Hawk. They got up to look at the cake.

"Wait," Hawk said. "Is that what I think it is?"

Nikki regained her voice. "Yes, it is," she replied.

The cake was three tiered. It had dark chocolate frosting with white highlights. Nikki knew without tasting it that Sylvia had gotten the flavor combination that Nikki had been looking for. The top of the cake was a reproduction of the cabin where Hawk had proposed to Nikki. The cabin and lake were all made out of chocolate and homemade candies. The forest around the lake was made of chocolate and the lake itself was made out of melted blue candy. The boat on the lake looked too good to eat. By the lake on the dock there was a bride and a groom. Nikki's eyes filled with tears.

"It's perfect," she whispered. Then she turned to Hawk.

"Surprise," she said.

Hawk smiled. "I love it! It looks too pretty to eat," he said.

"There is a reason the cabin is on the cake," Nikki said.

"Why is that?" Hawk asked.

"We need to live somewhere. Your house is too small and mine is too new for you," Nikki said. "I thought we could make the lake house our home. That is, if it's okay with the chief."

"Here are the keys," the chief said. "She's all yours." Hawk pulled Nikki close and kissed her deeply. Everyone cheered.

Nikki and Hawk cut the cake. It was marble cake with raspberries mixed into the batter. There was a small layer of raspberry sauce underneath the top layer of frosting. The cake was delicious. Nikki was overjoyed, and Hawk could not stop praising the flavor.

"This is incredible," Hawk said.

"You need to thank Sylvia," Nikki said.

"Nonsense," Sylvia replied. "All the credit goes to you. You designed the cake and practically wrote all the recipes for the cake and decorations. I just followed your instructions."

"Nikki, this is the best cake I have ever had. Thank you for making this so special," Hawk said. Nikki smiled. She thanked Seth, Lidia, and Tori for getting everything together. Nikki also thanked the mayor and his wife for providing the reception area and overseeing the wedding. A band started playing, and Hawk asked Nikki to dance.

Nikki and Hawk danced slowly around the dance floor. Hawk held his bride tight and made sure she did not hurt her ankle, but that did not stop him from dipping Nikki at the end of the dance.

After a while, Nikki told Hawk she was ready to leave. They hugged everyone goodbye and got into Hawk's car. They drove up the winding roads surrounded by evergreens to the lake house. Nikki saw a light in the distance. She figured the chief had turned on all the lights for them. Nikki was stunned to see it all lit up by candlelight.

"It's beautiful," Nikki gasped.

"You are not the only one who gets to surprise someone," Hawk said. "I have to confess my dad told me what you had planned, so I thought I'd get the cabin ready for us." He picked up Nikki and carried her across the threshold. He held her close and kissed her. Hawk led Nikki back outside to the fire pit and told her to sit down. Nikki sat and Hawk disappeared. He reappeared with wine and cheese.

"I thought you could use a bit more food," Hawk said.

"This is perfect," Nikki replied. They sat by the fire and sipped their wine. Nikki rested her head against Hawk's chest. She felt safe and secure. She also felt something she had not felt in a long time. She felt at home. Hawk took Nikki's almost empty glass from her hand. He slid his hand along the back of her neck and pulled her to his lips. Nikki kissed Hawk and felt warm and happy. Hawk leaned back. He stood up and scooped Nikki off of the bench. Nikki laughed. Hawk started to walk toward the water.

"Wait, what are you doing?" Nikki asked. She was happy but a little apprehensive. Hawk walked near the edge of the pier.

"Hawk, don't you dare!" Nikki shrieked.

Hawk laughed and turned around. "Would you rather go upstairs to bed?" he asked.

"I thought you'd never ask," Nikki replied.

Hawk carried her upstairs into her new and exciting life.

more from wendy

Alaska Cozy Mystery Series

Maple Hills Cozy Series

Sweeetfern Harbor Cozy Series

Sweet Peach Cozy Series

Sweet Shop Cozy Series

Twin Berry Bakery Series

about wendy meadows

Wendy Meadows is a USA Today bestselling author whose stories showcase women sleuths. To date, she has published dozens of books, which include her popular Sweetfern Harbor series, Sweet Peach Bakery series, and Alaska Cozy series, to name a few. She lives in the "Granite State" with her husband, two sons, two mini pigs and a lovable Labradoodle.

Join Wendy's newsletter to stay up-to-date with new releases. As a subscriber, you'll also get BLACKVINE MANOR, the complete series, for FREE!

Join Wendy's Newsletter Here
wendymeadows.com/cozy